FOREVER SURPRISED

FOREVER BLUEGRASS #6

KATHLEEN BROOKS

LAUREN PUBLISHING

Bluegrass Series

Bluegrass State of Mind

Risky Shot

Dead Heat

Bluegrass Brothers

Bluegrass Undercover

Rising Storm

Secret Santa: A Bluegrass Series Novella

Acquiring Trouble

Relentless Pursuit

Secrets Collide

Final Vow

Bluegrass Singles

All Hung Up

Bluegrass Dawn

The Perfect Gift

The Keeneston Roses

Forever Bluegrass Series

Forever Entangled

Forever Hidden

Forever Betrayed

Forever Driven

Forever Secret

Forever Concealed - coming September 19, 2017

Women of Power Series

Chosen for Power

Built for Power

Fashioned for Power

Destined for Power

Web of Lies Series

Whispered Lies

Rogue Lies

Shattered Lies - coming October 19, 2017

1

___

KENNA MASON ASHTON looked over the bench at the town's longest-running offender—a chronic public masturbator. Father Ben stood next to the offender, Mr. Chapman, as the young priest struggled not to laugh. Kenna was experiencing déjà vu. When she'd first arrived in Keeneston almost thirty-four years before, Father James had been the one standing next to Mr. Chapman, one of the first men she prosecuted. And here Chapman stood—again—with a different priest.

"What did you do now?" Kenna looked down at the man she had sadly gotten to know very well over the years.

His hair had turned a light brown with age, and there was a little bald ring on the crown of his head. "I was just so upset, Kenna . . . I mean, Judge Ashton."

Father Ben, a young, sinfully handsome priest in his early thirties, cleared his throat. She'd heard the stories of her daughter's friends mistakenly hitting on him and couldn't blame them in the least. Especially since he wore regular clothes most of the time. "Mr. Chapman was going to be meeting with me for counseling."

"But . . .?" Kenna knew something involving this man's penis would be an issue somehow.

"I didn't know they'd be there," Mr. Chapman sputtered. "Really. If I did, then I wouldn't have whipped it out."

"Who was there?" Kenna asked with dread.

"The nuns," Father Ben answered as he bit his lower lip to prevent himself from laughing out loud.

"Deputy Gray was showing them around town as a favor for Father Ben," Mr. Chapman began. "As you know, I've been doing real well with the whole public masturbating thing ever since I bought that farm out in the country. I can masturbate outside all the time and no one will see—on the tractor, baling hay, by the stream, or just sitting on my deck. But, I was real upset like, and so I went to see Father Ben."

"And?" Kenna urged him to get to the point.

"Well, my wife decided she wanted to move back in with me." Mr. Chapman didn't need to finish that explanation. His wife was a real ball-buster. The best thing that ever happened was when they separated ten years before. She'd moved to some compound or something in the mountains to live with more like-minded people. Some might call it a cult. It was a group that never smiled and disapproved of everything and everyone. Mr. Chapman and the town had greatly improved during her absence. Kenna cringed with the news she was coming back.

"Well, Father Ben was running late, and there's that fountain in the gardens behind the church. It's real soothing, and . . . well . . . the nuns," Mr. Chapman said as an explanation as he hung his head.

"Are the nuns all right?" Kenna asked Father Ben.

"Oh yes," Father Ben nodded. "In fact, they asked that charges not be pressed. Cody, I mean Deputy Gray, hauled

Mr. Chapman away before they could tell him not to. Apparently Mr. Chapman made quite an impression."

Kenna wanted to bang her head with the gavel. Instead she looked down at Mr. Chapman's hanging head. "Henry," she called out to the lawyer in the shiny silver suit talking to the group of other lawyers waiting their turn.

Henry Rooney's head popped up. "Yes, Judge?"

"You're practicing family law now, right?"

"Sure am."

"Mr. Chapman, the charges are dropped. I want you to seek counseling with Father Ben and Henry Rooney, or any lawyer of your choice, to discuss the return of your wife and the implications it could have on your criminal history. Dismissed." Kenna rapped her gavel.

Henry shivered. "She makes my balls run and hide."

"Mine too," Mr. Chapman muttered. "And I was so looking forward to doing something nice for the Rose sisters' hundredth birthday. But now I'm so upset all I want to do is—"

"We know what you want to do, Mr. Chapman," Kenna said, cutting him off. "But what did you say about the Rose sisters?"

The Rose sisters were elderly triplets who ran Keeneston from the Blossom Café. There wasn't a person in Keeneston who didn't owe something to the loveable, yet completely meddling, sisters.

"I thought to do something special for their hundredth birthday. It's in a couple days. Or at least it might be," Mr. Chapman explained. "I'm having a really hard time nailing down exactly which year they were born. I'm going with them being anywhere from ninety to a hundred twenty. But with the wife coming back . . ." Mr. Chapman and most of the people in the courtroom shivered.

"I knew their birthday was in a couple days, but I didn't know they were a hundred," Kenna muttered as the courtroom began to empty.

"I mean, I think they are," Mr. Chapman answered, seemingly not wanting to leave with the others. "Kenna, do you think it's wrong to get a divorce?"

Kenna walked back into her chambers with Mr. Chapman and Henry following. "I think it's a sin not to in your case," Henry answered for him. "Shoot, I'll do this one for free if you think she'll leave town again."

"Really?" Mr. Chapman perked up.

Kenna stopped listening as she unzipped her robe. "We have to do something special for them."

"For Mrs. Chapman? Something special would be sending her back into the mountains to live miles from any other living soul," Henry said as he perched himself at the edge of her desk.

"No," Kenna said with a roll of her eyes. "The Rose sisters. If it's their hundredth birthday, we need to celebrate." Kenna tapped her fingers on her desk as she thought. These ladies were the reason she was who she was. They were the heart and soul of the town. They did things for everyone, and now it was time for the town to say thank you.

"A surprise party!" Kenna gasped. "We'll throw a surprise party!"

"Can there be strippers? My wife hates nudity. I'm afraid I won't see another pair of boobies until . . ."

Kenna shooed Mr. Chapman and Henry from her office. She had a surprise birthday party to plan, and she knew exactly who to ask for help.

There was nothing Kenna loved more than walking up Main Street in Keeneston. In an era when people were glued to their phones as they walked down the street, Keeneston fought against the changing times. In some ways, that is. In other ways, they were miles ahead in technology. After all, they had a gossip text hotline. But when not reporting gossip, people waved, stopped you to chat for a moment, and cars honked their hellos as they drove by. Doors to the shops were propped open, inviting one and all to step inside for a bit. Then there was the smell of the cooking from the Blossom Café.

The Blossom Café was across the street from the courthouse and packed as people gathered for lunch. All of downtown was historic, but the café held a special place in everyone's heart. The three-story, pale yellow brick building with a purple door and a large plate glass window overlooking Main Street was gossip central. Daisy Mae Rose and Violet Fae Rose opened it decades ago and had since retired and passed the daily operations over to their much younger cousins, Poppy and Zinnia Meadows. Miss Lily Rae Rose ran the bed and breakfast, and that too was now under Poppy and Zinnia's control.

Although the delicious smells coming from the café were enough to make her think twice of delaying her plans, Kenna turned from the café and headed up Main Street. The street was lined with dark purples, hot pinks, and bright white flowers in baskets attached to the light posts. American flags waved in the breeze and there were pretty benches for those who wanted to sit and chat with the passers-by.

Kenna smiled at the bank teller heading to lunch. She waved through the open window at her insurance agent.

She stopped to check out the new piece hanging in the window of the art studio and smiled at the line of women waiting for their turn to have their hair and nails done at the Fluff and Buff.

It only took a couple of minutes to reach her destination at the other end of Main Street. Kenna pushed open the door to Southern Charms and a bell rang. The warm shop, painted in yellows and whites and accented in blues, was filled with people taking advantage of Paige Davies Parker's annual one-day hat sale. Paige was a famous hat designer. And once a year, she put all of her hats on sale to make room for the new styles.

Paige had been her best friend since Kenna's frantic escape for her life in New York City. She had been chased, hunted, and eventually found. She had met Paige on the road to Keeneston, and they'd been friends ever since. Even when Dani, Kenna's best friend and paralegal from New York City, arrived, it was as if the three of them were inseparable. They'd been through love, attempted murder, a trial that captivated the tabloids, and children, and now were united in their quest to become grandparents. Each of them had one child married, but no grandbabies, much to their disappointment. However, the grandbaby hunt needed to be put on hold for a while as she caught Paige's eye and motioned for her to join her behind the counter.

Kenna pulled her auburn hair out of the French twist and rubbed her head as she waited for her friend to join her. Paige finished answering questions for a group of women and walked toward Kenna with a huge smile on her face. Her brown hair had lightened with age, but she had the same happy-go-lucky smile she'd had since they'd met. Her hazel eyes twinkled as if she were in on a secret joke.

"Hey! Looking for a hat?" Paige asked as she stepped behind the counter to meet Kenna.

Kenna shook her head. "It's about the Rose sisters."

Paige's smile dropped. "Are they okay?"

"Yes, but did you know the day after tomorrow is their hundredth birthday?"

Paige's eyes rounded. "Is that how old they are?"

"Well," Kenna shrugged. "That's the best Mr. Chapman can figure."

"I thought for sure they were a hundred five," Paige chuckled.

"I want to throw a surprise birthday party for them. What do you think?" Kenna asked as a couple of women stopped at the counter to pay for hats.

"I think that's a great idea. But there's no way we can pull off a surprise party. You forget Miss Lily is married to John Wolfe, and John knows everything before it even happens. Aliens. I'm positive."

The door opened and Kenna saw Aniyah strut in. Aniyah's mocha skin was glistening from the summer heat and an apparent run down Main Street in her signature five-inch heels. Without them, Aniyah was the height of a fifth grader with the body of a pinup. Her black hair was styled perfectly and held in place with a diamond clip. Her generous curves were on full display and her hoop earrings were so big the basketball team could shoot through them.

"I heard we're throwing a surprise party," she panted as she ignored the visitors and tourists and made her way around the counter.

Paige gave Kenna an "I told you so" look.

"John?" Paige asked, not surprised the news was already spreading.

"What? Oh, no. DeAndre just told me."

Paige shook her head. "Do aliens talk to him like we think they talk to John? Because I can't think of any other way those two men know what's going on so fast."

"I don't think so, but I just watched this show about aliens. Did you know there could be aliens among us right now?" Aniyah asked, dropping her voice and looking around suspiciously at the people in the shop.

Kenna stared at the young woman in her early twenties and didn't know what to say. It was a joke that aliens talked to John, well, half joke and half serious. How else could he get all his gossip? It was a complete unknown. The town hadn't seen anything like it until DeAndre Drews and his girlfriend came to town almost a year before. In under a week, DeAndre was scooping John on gossip. Kenna thought DeAndre wiretapped the town somehow, and maybe John did too. But while John was analog, DeAndre was digital.

"Well, however DeAndre found out, make sure he doesn't tell anyone," Kenna scolded as if Aniyah were one of her children.

"Of course not. I want to help."

Kenna thought for a second. "You can be the distraction. On their birthday, in the afternoon, why don't you take them to the Fluff and Buff? And afterward, you'll have to make a quick stop at my house. That's where we can have the party."

"Oh, I know!" Paige practically bounced. "I'll take something down to the Fluff and Buff and see if I can talk you all into delivering it out to Kenna or Will. If anyone can talk the Rose sisters into a quick trip out to Kenna's, it's you."

"I can do that. Now, did you save that hat for me?"

Kenna left with Aniyah and her new purchase. Aniyah went to conspire with Nora, the owner of the Fluff and Buff, while Kenna went to meet Dani. Together, they would make sure the whole town was ready for the most epic birthday party in Keeneston history.

2

KENNA LOOKED across the coffee table at her two best friends and raised her glass of wine. "Then we have a plan," Kenna said as they toasted.

Dani's long dark hair was pulled back into a ponytail as she took a sip of her wine. "How are things going with Sienna and Ryan?" she asked their mothers. Kenna's daughter had married Paige's son almost four years earlier.

Paige and Kenna shared a look of exasperation. "Still no grandbaby," Kenna complained.

"I keep leaving baby items on their porch in hopes it'll give them ideas," Paige winked.

Dani laughed and shook her head.

"Oh, as if you're innocent," Kenna teased.

"What is my wife innocent of?" Mo asked as he came in and kissed Dani on the cheek.

"Well, we know we aren't talking about my wife then," Cole Parker joked as he strode in behind Mo. Kenna's husband, Will, was next. Paige swatted her husband and Cole pretended injury before bending down to kiss her.

"Did you know it was the Rose sisters' hundredth birthday in two days?" Kenna asked Will.

"Wow, no. I had no idea how old they were."

"We didn't either. And we're not really sure, but it's Mr. Chapman's best guess," Kenna told them.

"Best guess?" Cole asked.

Kenna cringed. "Well, their past driver's licenses all had different years of birth on them. Mr. Chapman pulled the high school yearbooks and talked to Jake and Marcy, along with Will's parents, and we're pretty sure it's their hundredth birthday. Give or take a year or two."

"So we've decided to host a surprise party!" Paige finished telling them.

"How are you going to pull that off?" Mo asked. "We still have some decorations up from Sophie and Nash's wedding that we could use."

"We thought about that," Kenna explained. "But every time we have a town function, you all host it. We thought they may get suspicious if we have them driving up to your house. Instead, I thought we'd have it at our house."

Her husband raised his brows in thought. "Why don't we have it at the main house? You know my parents are moving to Florida at the end of the month. I'm sure they'd love to host one last blowout at their house."

"I'm going to miss William and Betsy," Paige said sadly. "What are you going to do with the main house?"

Will sat down next to his wife and rested his hand on her thigh. All these years and she was still madly in love with her football-obsessed husband. "Since Will has taken to playing owner and general manager of the Lexington Thoroughbreds' football team, Carter has had to step up and manage the farm. He's been commuting every day from the house he owns on the other side of Keeneston. Not that it's far, but we thought we'd move into the main house and let Carter move into ours. Ryan and Sienna are already settled and maybe this might encourage Carter to do the same." Kenna thought about her son. It would be hard leaving the house that she and Will had raised their children in, but Carter was a man now. His thirtieth birthday was coming up. It was time he settled down and started a family. Sienna and Ryan hadn't started their family yet, and she didn't think Carter would be the kind to skip to the head of that line.

"Yeah, Mom and Dad found a great house down the street from Judge Cooper, Edna, and Tabby." Will tried to sound upbeat about his parents moving, but Kenna knew it was bothering him.

"They'll have a great time there," Mo said, nodding his head. "What is Carter up to on that farm of yours?" he asked, changing the subject.

"He's breeding his first season of mares all on his own and has a couple of two-year-olds he's really optimistic about," Will said of their son. Kenna was so proud of their boy. He'd taken over managing the farm with ease. Now if only his personal life would run as smoothly. "How's your brood doing?" Will asked Mo and Dani.

"Don't get me started on that son of mine," Dani complained.

Cole snickered. "Which one?"

"Gabriel." Dani shook her head. "I swear he purposely finds paparazzi when he has the bimbo of the day on his arm."

"We hope he'll settle down once he's given more responsibility," Mo explained. "My brother, the king, will be at the charity ball in a couple weeks with an assignment for him."

"Sounds ominous." Will smiled at the their longtime friends.

"It won't be easy. But hopefully the effects of his behavior will be eye-opening," Mo explained.

"And Ariana? How is she enjoying D.C.?" Paige asked about Mo and Dani's youngest.

"She loves it. Abby is showing her the ropes around town," Dani said with joy clearly showing on her face. "I know Jackson is off with the FBI. What is Greer doing this summer?"

"As you know, she graduated from college last month. She will travel for part of the summer and then we don't know. She says she'll work something out. I'll message them both to see if they can fly in for the party." Paige pulled out her phone and sent a text to her children.

Cole grinned proudly. "I think Greer is being recruited by the FBI."

Paige rolled her eyes. "Can you imagine? All of my children in the FBI?"

"Well, you did teach them to shoot, and your husband was the head of the FBI here until he retired and Ryan took over. At this point, it's a family tradition," Kenna pointed out.

This time it was Paige who grinned proudly. "I did teach them to shoot. Greer can outshoot her brothers and her father."

"Cole should have more time to practice now that he's retired," Will taunted.

"Ha!" Paige smacked her husband's arm. "He's not retired. He's decided to help me run my shop. He bought a barcode scanner to, quote, 'help me with inventory' for Mother's Day."

"It was top of the line," Cole defended before getting

smacked again. "What? Your store is still going strong, and you even have a television crew coming at the end of the year to see how you start making hats for the Derby."

"Wow, that's great!" the group all said to Paige.

"Yup, now all I need is a grandchild," Paige said longingly.

"Don't we all?" Dani agreed. "But back to the Rose sisters. We need to call in reinforcements to pull this off. And invitations have to be sent out via text since we're running short on time."

Kenna nodded her head in agreement. "And because the postman is one of their informants."

"He is?" Cole said, surprised.

"Duh. How else did the Rose sisters know you got a vasectomy? The postman told them about the bill you got in the mail." Paige was still mortified about them announcing to the entire café that Cole had been snipped and that was almost two decades ago. It was still the same postman who delivered mail, so texting was their only option.

"Then let's get to work," Kenna said, rubbing her hands together and pulling out a notebook.

3

CADE DAVIES LOOKED across the dinner table at his wife and smiled. He'd spent the day with his brothers at his parents' farm mending fences. During that time they'd talked.

"I told them my son-in-law was the biggest badass in town. Deacon and Matt are good men, but Nash—he's a badass."

Annie made an *hmmm* sound in agreement as she chewed her food. It was a common discussion around their dinner table.

"Miles then said Layne would never get married, and we teased him that was because no man could stand up to a Miles glare. But Nash could. I made sure to point that out."

Annie made her *hmmm* noise again so Cade continued on. "Oh, and I hope you don't mind, but all the brothers decided on another guys' trip. I think we're going to go camping. Do a little fishing. That kind of thing."

"*Hmmm*," Annie said again as she took a sip of her wine. "Good. Bridget and I were thinking of a spa weekend anyway. Just let me know when you plan on going and we'll make our plans." Annie thought about telling her husband she knew their brothers' trips were code for him, Miles, Marshall, and Cy going on missions for the government, but then she might have to tell Cade her spa weekends with Bridget were working with the DEA and decided against it.

Cade, Miles, and Marshall were retired Special Forces while Cy had been a spy. Other men's midlife crises involved buying a sports car or dating a twenty-year-old, so in the grand scheme of things, going on missions for Special Forces, or the CIA, or whoever needed them, wasn't a big deal. Especially when Annie herself was back working undercover for the DEA. Not that she didn't feel fulfilled as a sheriff's deputy, but she got to shoot more people with the DEA.

"Why don't you take Colton and Landon?" Annie asked, just to mess with him. Their sons would be less interested in going than Cade and his brothers would be in having them cover up the fact they were working with the government again.

"Uh, they wouldn't want to hang out with us old guys. I'm sure they're busy with their last real summer together now that Colton has graduated from college. Before we know it, Colton will be training at the National Fire Academy and Landon will be in his last year of college," Cade said, knowing it would get his wife talking about their sons.

"I can't believe Colton has done so much already. By the time he's twenty-five, he's going to be in charge of FEMA's emergency response team for our area and probably the fire station as well," Annie said with wonder.

During college, Colton realized he excelled at quick thinking and the ability to organize people just as quickly after he'd evacuated the science lab when it caught on fire. He wanted to join FEMA or become a firefighter. When he looked into it, he discovered Keeneston and neighboring Lipston had no emergency coordinator, even though there was a hundred-thousand-acre forest in the counties. There was also no full-time fire department in Keeneston, only a small volunteer one.

Taking charge, Colton pleaded to the Keeneston town council to open a fire department. They couldn't afford it but gave Colton their blessing to start one if he could find the funding and become certified. He agreed to get the training and to form an emergency response team along with the fire department. The reasoning was the federal forest had no fire department to service it. After a fire had broken out the previous summer, they realized they needed protection for the campers and hikers who were regularly in the forest. As such, he bid on a contract to be the civilian fire department for the forest and won it along with a construction grant from the federal government. In return, when the Keeneston Fire Department was up and running, they would be on call for FEMA emergencies as well. He was given one year to get a fire station in operation. So far, he was recruiting people from the area and all over the country to fill the department.

"We did good on the kid department." Cade winked. "When does Sophie get back from her honeymoon?" he asked.

"Tomorrow at five," Annie answered as she reached for her phone and read the incoming text message. "Oh my goodness."

"What is it?"

"It's from Kenna. In two days it's the Rose sisters' hundredth birthday, and they're going to throw a surprise party for them at William and Betsy's house. She's asked for you and your brothers to provide the meat for the town and for all the sisters-in-law to bake desserts."

Cade nodded. "We can do that. Each brother can provide a steer. That should feed the town."

"Apparently I am in charge of apple pies."

"It's because your ass is shaped like an apple. I can't wait to take a bite out of you tonight." Annie rolled her eyes. Married thirty years and he was still as randy as a college man. Not that she was complaining . . . at all.

Marshall tossed his dust-covered cowboy hat on the kitchen table and kicked off his boots, sending dirt and dust onto the floor. Who knew retirement was more work than when he was sheriff? He was thinking of asking Matt for his job back if it got him out of running multiple farms.

Walking through the kitchen, he gave his vizsla, Robert, a scratch behind the ear and a bone for his long day of work beside Marshall and his brothers at their parents' farm. Robert took his bone and plopped onto the couch to enjoy it as Marshall headed for the shower.

He heard the water running when he entered his bedroom and smiled. His wife was home. And naked. And wet. Quickly stripping, Marshall strode into the bathroom. He watched Katelyn soap her body through the glass door and grinned. He was one lucky son of a bitch.

Katelyn didn't even look surprised as he slid into the shower with her. "Hey honey. How are things at your parents'?"

"Good. The fences are all fixed, and I didn't kill Cade when he said Nash was a bigger badass than Deacon." His son-in-law was an investigator. While he didn't kill as many people as Nash, he kept their daughter Sydney safe and happy. To Marshall, that was a win. Okay, it wouldn't hurt if he shot a couple more people, but he was still young and in Keeneston. You never know what might happen next.

Katelyn rose up and pressed her soapy body against his and kissed him until all thoughts of the battle of the sons-in-law were gone.

"How was your day?" Marshall asked, taking over washing his wife's body.

"Good. Had to help Wyatt this afternoon with a foal that was stuck. It was a nice change from delivering puppies. But way messier. And smellier."

"Good thing I'm here to help then." Marshall spun her around and began to soap her front.

"I don't deliver foals with my breasts, honey," Katelyn teased until her laughter turned to a moan of delight. Marshall smirked. He still had it.

Thirty minutes later they were both clean and dressing when their son, Wyatt, called to report the foal was doing well. Katelyn was a small-animal veterinarian and their son had chosen to become a large-animal vet. He was a damn good one, too, but since they were the only doctors in their practice, sometimes they helped each other out. It made his wife happy to work with her son after spending his younger years traveling so much with Sydney when she had modeling shoots. But Sydney had left modeling behind just as Katelyn had. When Katelyn went into veterinary medicine, Syd had gone into business. She owned a fashion house offering clothing, furniture, and accessories.

Their phones buzzed before Marshall could tell her about Miles saying his daughter Layne would never get married. Marshall looked at the text. "Did you get this about the Rose sisters?"

"Yes, I'm supposed to bake cupcakes."

"I'm bringing a steer."

"What a great idea. I thought the Rose sisters turned a hundred years ago." Katelyn shrugged. "We're meeting at Kenna's house tomorrow afternoon to start decorating after we bake."

"The guys and I will transport the steers to the butcher in the morning and then start smoking the meat. This should be fun if we can pull it off, but you know the Rose sisters," Marshall said over his shoulder as the two of them headed downstairs for dinner.

"We can do it. They'll never see it coming," Katelyn grinned mischievously as her mind was already running through the list of things she needed to get.

~

"We'll never pull this off," Morgan Davies told her husband, Miles, as they sat on the couch.

"If I can plan a secret rescue operation of an American hostage, then I can plan and execute a surprise party for the Rose sisters," Miles told his wife as he pulled her to him. She rested her head on him and absently ran her fingers over his chest. Her dark hair was now streaked with silver, but Morgan was still the most beautiful woman he'd ever seen.

"When did you plan that?"

Damn. She was also a very clever wife. That rescue mission was done after his supposed retirement from the Special Forces. But after their daughter, Layne, moved out, he needed a hobby.

It turned out his brothers felt the same, so they'd called up their old commander who happened to be their friend Bridget's dad. They worked out like madmen and two months later took their first guys' trip was to Fort Bragg in North Carolina to show those young men a thing or two. They passed their physical and mental evaluations with flying colors and were certified as Army Civilian Contractors. They took the assignments they wanted and turned down the ones they didn't. It was the perfect job, even if Miles was still running his farm co-op company and his brothers were still working the farms. It was something to do on the weekends.

"Hmm, a lifetime ago now. I'm sure I told you that story," he told his wife before describing the hostage rescue he and his brothers organized and assisted with just a couple of years ago. Speaking of Layne, Miles grabbed his phone and pulled up the app to check on her whereabouts. He wanted to make sure she was home safe and sound. He wasn't sure if his wife believed him or not, but then she looked up and caught him checking on Layne and all talk of hostage rescue was forgotten.

"I thought you promised to stop spying on our daughter! Miles, she's a grown woman."

"She's my little girl," Miles defended.

Morgan pushed off his chest and looked over at him. "Miles, you taught her twenty-five ways to kill someone with her bare hands. I'm pretty sure she's safe."

"You didn't see the way I took that boy down at Sophie and Nash's wedding. It was beautiful. Him thinking he could dance that closely to my daughter and then minutes later shaking as he ran from me. She still needs me to protect her."

Morgan shook her head. "She's lonely. She's lonely because you're scaring all the men away."

Miles grunted. He didn't want his baby lonely, but he also didn't want her stuck with some wimp she couldn't respect either. "She has us. Besides, if he runs screaming, he's not the right man. When one comes along who doesn't run, I'll welcome him to the family. And then I can finally shove it down Cade's throat that my son-in-law is the biggest badass."

Morgan smiled radiantly as her hair curtained his face. "That's the sexiest thing I have ever heard."

"That I want my son-in-law to be a bigger badass than Nash?"

"That you want a son-in-law. Oh, think, Miles. Layne as a mother and our grandchildren running around the farm. I could retire from the PR company and stop managing crises in order to help babysit for Layne while she's at work. We tried for so long to have another child and it just wasn't meant to be. But to have grandchildren—" Morgan sighed.

Miles wanted to growl. Didn't she know how grandbabies were made? Although, a sweet little girl with hazel eyes and bouncing curls whom he could teach self-defense . . . maybe it wouldn't be so bad.

4

"PIERCE!" Tammy cried as she read the text from Kenna. "Did you get a text about the Rose sisters' birthday party?"

"I don't have my phone, sweetheart," Pierce called from his workshop. He was tinkering with a new idea to help keep soil full of nutrients so crops would grow bigger, better, and faster. He heard his wife's footsteps hurry through the kitchen and out into his workshop.

His wife rushed into the large room filled with countless tools, building materials, and everything in between. Pierce and Tammy could have retired a long time ago. The amount of money he made on his Cropbot was enough to live a lifetime on. However, his inventions weren't about money. They were ideas that came to him to improve farming so farmers could grow better produce and live a more financially secure life. And when it came down to it, he and Tammy weren't made for retirement. At least not yet.

However, they'd begun to plan. She was still working for Henry Rooney part-time as a paralegal. They'd talked about stepping back a little in order to travel the world. He and Tammy had always focused on work and raising four children. Now that the youngest, Cassidy, was off at college, it was time for him and his wife to have some new adventures.

"What was the text?" he asked as Tammy held out his phone to him. She pulled the phone back and started talking. She was so excited she was practically bouncing.

"Kenna, Dani, and Paige are hosting a surprise one hundredth birthday party for the Rose sisters in two days!"

Pierce put down the wrench and wiped the grease on his jeans. "Wow, the Rose sisters are turning one hundred?" Pierce grinned as he looked at one of his discarded projects in the far corner of the room. "I have the perfect gift for them."

Tammy shook her head. "Those things go faster than an ATV. You can't give them to three little old ladies!"

"They'll love it. What are we supposed to do for this party?" Pierce asked, already thinking of some modifications he needed to make for the electric scooters.

"I'm supposed to bake five hundred cookies by tomorrow night, and you're supposed to bring enough corn on the cob for the entire town," Tammy told him. Her small, fairylike face crunched up as she thought. "I think I'll call the principal and see if the sisters-in-law can bake at the school tomorrow. I'll start tonight at home, but using the commercial kitchen can really speed things along."

"Good idea. What is everyone else bringing?"

"Your brothers are bringing the meat. Miles just texted you and your brothers. They're meeting at six in the morning to take the steers to the butchers. Then each of the sisters-in-law is baking desserts or appetizers. It's going to be at William and Betsy's house. Aniyah is in charge of getting them there."

"We need to call the kids and see if they can make it,"

Pierce said, taking his phone from Tammy. "The Rose sisters mean so much to them. They'll be disappointed if they're not here."

"Piper will be able to make it," Tammy said, nodding as she sent their eldest child a text about the party. Piper was living in Keeneston but owned a private nanotechnology lab in Lexington as well as being a founding scientist for the Rahmi International Lab. Piper was tall with dirty blonde hair and the signature Davies hazel eyes. It was the exact opposite of Tammy. Tammy was five-one on a good day with light blonde hair and wasn't scientifically inclined at all. Piper, on the other hand, inherited her desire to work with viruses and nanotech from her father. Tammy looked down at her phone. "Piper is in. Kenna has already asked her to bring napkins."

Pierce sent a text to their youngest. Piper and Cassidy were always the easiest to get hold of. Cassidy was interning for the summer at the university in Lexington, teaching German and French. While not science-based like Pierce, Cassidy had an ear for languages and could become fluent in a new language in mere months. "Cassidy said she can make it, and she's in charge of streamers and balloons."

"Now let's see if we can find our two sons," Tammy chuckled. Dylan, their second-born child and eldest son, never told them what he did for a living. Tammy knew it was military-based. Wasn't hard to determine that when he'd disappear with no notice for an undetermined length of time and had a body his Uncle Miles would have been jealous of during his time in the Special Forces. Tammy just prayed her baby would make it home every time he disappeared. She had faith in him, though. He may be quiet, but he was a fierce protector. And it was better for him to do this when he was still young, only twenty-six years old, and then settle down rather than having a midlife crisis and doing something dangerous like her husband and his brothers were doing. Of course, Pierce wasn't Special Forces so he was the decoy. He took the worst doctored photos imaginable to prove they were fishing or skiing during their brothers' trips.

And then there was Jace. Her sweet boy was in medical school after coming back from a humanitarian trip in Africa. He wanted to join an emergency response medical team. Unfortunately, that meant he'd be traveling all over the world. Which is what had given her and Pierce the idea to begin stepping back from their jobs and traveling themselves.

"I'll call Jace. You try to get hold of Dylan," Tammy said, calling her son.

"Hello," came the tired voice.

"Oh, sweetheart, I'm sorry I woke you. I was wondering if you got a text from Kenna?"

"Hold on," Jace mumbled. He was in Chicago working with doctors to vaccinate children and provide heath care to those without the means to do so. He worked all hours of the day and night. "I see it. I think I can make it. I was supposed to have two days off a week ago and never took them. Then I'm supposed to have another two days off starting tomorrow but was called in to help. I'll see if I can work a half day tomorrow and then come home for a couple days."

Tammy did a little happy dance. She loved having all her babies under her roof again. "Your father and I can't wait to see you. I'll let you get back to sleep. We love you."

"Love you too, Ma."

Tammy looked at Pierce sending a text. "Anything from Dylan?"

Pierce shook his head. "But I know how to find him."

"No!" Tammy lunged for the phone. "You can't call John Wolfe. He might let it slip to Miss Lily about the party."

"I wasn't going to call John. I was going to call DeAndre. He's freaky fast at finding this stuff. I think he has access to NSA servers or something."

Pierce sent a text to DeAndre and then slipped his hand around his wife. "Why don't I help you with the cookies? Let me program the corn picker and it'll pick enough corn for the party by the morning."

"You know I can't resist a man in the kitchen," Tammy teased.

Pierce winked. "I know. Why do you think I help cook so much?"

Tammy laughed as she headed for the kitchen while Pierce scheduled the machinery to pick the corn. Ten minutes later, Pierce had his arms around her from behind as she mixed the batter. His hands roamed her body as she put in the chocolate chips. "I know what we can do while the first batch is in the oven," he whispered in her ear as his hand showed her exactly what he meant.

"Too bad your phone is ringing," Tammy said, looking over her shoulder and kissing her husband.

Pierce grabbed the phone. "It's Dylan," he said, surprised. "Hey, son."

"I got an urgent message to call you. Are you guys okay?" His son's deep voice sounded far away.

"Yes. The town is throwing the Rose sisters a surprise hundredth birthday in two days. Your mother and I wanted to see if you could make it. Is that gunfire?" Pierce asked as his wife spun around and grabbed for the phone. Pierce put it on speakerphone.

"Yeah, I'm just playing a video game with my friend. He has killer surround sound," Dylan answered.

"Hi, honey," Tammy said as her hands twisted into her apron with worry.

"Hey, Mom. So the Rose sisters are turning one hundred? I thought they were older than that." Dylan chuckled as Pierce recognized the distraction.

"Where are you?" Pierce asked instead.

"At a friend's house," he said vaguely.

"Do you think you can make the party?" Tammy asked.

"Two days from now? I think I can. I'm helping my buddies with a project, and if we can get it finished, I'll be there. But they're waiting for me, so I better get going. Love you both."

"We love you too, son," Pierce told Dylan before the line went dead. His wife looked white as a sheet. "He'll be okay. Whatever he's doing, he's brave, strong, and smart. He'll come home to us."

Wrapping his wife in his arms, he felt her nod against his chest a moment before the first tear fell.

"Will it make you stop crying if I help you bake while wearing nothing but an apron?" His wife laughed.

"I do believe it would." Tammy sniffled as she dried her eyes.

"I'm always eager to please," Pierce said, wiggling his eyebrows and shoving his jeans to the floor.

"I thought I'd find you in here," Cy said, eyeing his wife from the patio door. Gemma was sitting on an outdoor lounge chair in the summer's night working on her laptop.

"Hold on. I just have to blow up a helicopter." Gemma's

fingers flew over the keyboard as her eyes never left the screen. His wife had been hit with a scene for her new book in the middle of dinner. She'd dropped her fork, shoved her chair from the table, and disappeared into the night to work.

Cy watched her brow wrinkle and then she gasped. Five minutes later, she finally appeared to breathe again.

"Ah, there was a time I remember actually blowing up a helicopter in real life," Cy sighed, remembering the glory days. Though he did get to fire an RPG during his last brothers' trip. Good times.

"I was so inspired by a story Layne told me about one of the veterans she was helping with physical therapy that a whole book developed on the spot," Gemma said, closing her laptop. "Sorry I ran out on dinner."

"It's okay. It's in the fridge for later. I thought you'd like to know there is going to be a surprise party for the Rose sisters' hundredth birthday in two days," Cy told her, taking a seat next to her.

"Wow! That's going to be so much fun. Who's putting it on?"

"Kenna, Dani, and Paige. Kenna texted that I'm to bring a steer and you are to bring five gallons of your famous potato salad." His wife blinked at the large number.

"Are we feeding the whole town?" Gemma asked.

"Sure are. The party is at William and Betsy's house. The entire town is invited."

"When do the boys get back from their rodeo?" Gemma asked as Cy held open the door for her.

"Probably around midnight. Why?" Cy asked.

"Does it look like I have seventy-five pounds of potatoes sitting around?" Gemma teased as she sent a text to her twin boys, Porter and Parker. "I'll have them pick up the potatoes on their way home so I can work on it all morning."

Cy leaned against the counter as his wife went through the kitchen and sent a grocery list to the boys.

The two brothers had just graduated from college and were spending the summer on the professional rodeo circuit, much to Gemma's displeasure. She believed they needed to get a real job—one that wasn't so dangerous.

"Hey, do you think something is up with Reagan?" Cy asked about his daughter as he looked down at his phone.

"Why do you ask?" Gemma called from the pantry. He and his wife had different opinions on how to look out for their twin daughters and Cy hesitated a moment too long in answering. "Are you tracking her again?"

"No," Cy said, turning off his cell phone. She'd managed to circumvent the tracking program he put on her cell. Right now it said she was in Italy. She should be at her house at the back of the farm that she used to share with her sister, Riley, before Riley had married and moved out.

"Cyland Davies. Reagan is almost thirty years old. You need to stop spying on her," Gemma said, coming out of the pantry with her hands on her hips. "I'll never get grandchildren if you keep this up. If I don't get grandchildren, I'll make you pay for it."

Cy was pretty sure the growling sound he heard was coming from him, but by the way his wife was staring him down he wasn't sure. He didn't want any man touching his daughters, even if that man happened to be her husband. His wife read his thoughts and rolled her eyes.

"I think the brothers are going on another guys' trip."

Gemma shook her head as she looked at her spice rack while Cy tried to distract her. "If you want adventure, why don't you start a private military or security firm or maybe a training facility? Isn't that what Abby does?"

Abby Mueez was Ahmed and Bridget's daughter. Ahmed

was an even scarier version of Cy. And that was very hard for Cy to admit. And Bridget was no slouch herself, having grown up and served in the military.

"So she says. The guys she brought with her when Sophie needed help were not private contractors. They had military stamped on their foreheads." Cy paused. "However, that's an interesting idea. The guys want to go camping so I'll bring it up and see what they say about it."

Bridget pulled back her right hand and slammed it into her husband. Ahmed absorbed the hit to his shoulder as his wife followed with a hook. He deflected the punch and swept her feet out from under her. She had seen it coming and had begun to jump, but Ahmed managed to snag a heel and that was all it took to send her off balance and falling to the matted floor of their workout room.

Bridget lay breathing heavily on the floor and smiled up at him. "I'll get you next time."

"I might just let you, depending on what we wager." Ahmed sent her a wink as he used his teeth to pull loosen the Velcro on the sparring gloves. In quick work, he placed his gloves on the bench and helped Bridget take hers off.

"Now for my prize." Ahmed pulled his wife in for a kiss, but they were interrupted by the constant buzzing on their phones.

"Hold on. My phone has been going crazy." Bridget gave her husband another quick kiss and reached for her phone. "Honey, it's the Rose sisters' hundredth birthday day after tomorrow."

Ahmed raised his eyebrow. "Are you sure about that? I'm pretty sure they're older than that."

"Don't you know better than to question a woman about her age?"

Ahmed knew better than to say anything in response. "What's the plan then?"

"The party will be at Ashton Farm. They gave us some things to get for tomorrow." Bridget handed him the phone to look at. "I bet Kale could get here for the party, but what about Abby?"

Ahmed grunted in response. His wife was used to his non-answers. "She should move home. I don't like her being so far away when using weapons."

"You mean you can't have a drone follow her anymore."

"She shot my last one down," Ahmed grumbled.

Bridget wrapped her arm around his and leaned against him. "I'm sorry, but I don't think she's ready to come home yet. And I know you're worried about her, but remember who taught her everything she knows—me," his wife teased as she looked up at him. "You'll have to be satisfied with Kale coming home after his internship."

"After his internship with the CIA, he won't be coming home. Not if they're smart. He has computer skills that Nash and Nabi could only dream of," Ahmed said with pride about his son.

"Yes, but Kale also likes to dance around the legal line. I'm guessing the government would frown on that."

"I wouldn't assume all government organizations would mind someone who could tiptoe around the law," Ahmed shrugged.

"None that would admit to it anyway, I guess," Bridget said, wiping her face with a towel.

Ahmed nodded. "Agreed. But cyber warfare is a dirty business. The people waging the war don't care for the laws, so you need someone who can play just as dirty on the good side."

Bridget sighed. "So what we're finally realizing is our birds have flown the nest. With that sad thought, I'm glad I have an upcoming spa trip with Annie. We can cry together that our children are all grown up."

"Oh," Ahmed said, trying to contain his pleasure, "you have a girls' trip? That's good, because Miles asked if I wanted to go camping with his brothers."

"Sure. Though I never knew you to be the camping type."

"Uh, well, remember that time I told you about having to hike across the Pakistani mountains while pursuing my target? Camping with the guys will be a luxury compared to that trip."

His wife didn't look convinced. "Whatever you say. I'll be relaxing in a seaweed wrap. But now we need to focus on the Rose sisters."

Ahmed pulled Bridget flush against him. "And I have a prize to claim."

5

TREY EVERETT CARRIED the heavy suitcase down the stairs and set it with the rest of the boxes and suitcases. His wife, Taylor, was running through the checklist of everything their youngest son, Knox, would need at summer football camp. In less than five days, their youngest would be off to college on a full football scholarship. Unlike Trey, who had been a running back for the Georgia Vultures in the NFL, Knox was one hell of a quarterback.

Trey looked at all the football gear, bedding, and electronics sitting by the garage door waiting to be loaded up. Trey began coaching after he retired as a player. He started off by coming back to Keeneston High School to coach, but when Mo Ali Rahman and Will Ashton, his football idol, started an NFL franchise in Lexington, they tapped Trey to become a coach. Will had played quarterback in the NFL and then had been one of Trey's high school coaches.

When Knox began to show interest in football, especially the quarterback position, Trey had asked Will to help him out. He did more than that. He had let Knox work out during some Thoroughbred practices, and as a result, Knox was looking at a starting position as a freshman come fall.

"I can't believe they'll both be gone," Taylor sighed. Knox was now eighteen and heading off to college while their elder son, Holt, was twenty and making a name for himself in Nashville as a country singer.

Trey kissed his wife's head and hugged her. She was still as beautiful as she was the first day he met her. She'd been a bouncy blonde knockout when she visited her "uncle" Cy in Keeneston. Cy had basically adopted the young actress when he was undercover as a stuntman in Hollywood. And luckily for Trey, that meant he got to know her outside of the Hollywood lights. They'd attended Vanderbilt together and then were married while he was playing for the Vultures. Taylor had taken some time off from acting here and there through the past twenty years, but as she got older her passion was turning solely to directing.

"We've done good, babe," Trey whispered into her hair. He didn't want to admit it, but he was feeling the loss of having both sons out of the house as well.

"Mom! Dad!" Knox called as all six feet four inches thundered down the stairs. "Did you get a text from Miss Kenna?"

"I haven't looked. I've been busy carrying your things downstairs," Trey said sarcastically. His son's exuberance was one of the things he loved best.

"What is it, dear?" Taylor asked, pulling her long blonde hair into a messy bun.

"They're throwing a surprise party for the Rose sisters' hundredth birthday in two days. I won't have to miss it! They asked me and the rest of the football team to help. I guess they have a tent, table, and chairs they need help setting up."

Trey and Taylor went into the living room to get their phones. "I'm to bring decorations. Cassidy is in charge of streamers and balloons, so I'll work with her on coordinating that."

Knox cleared his throat. "Um, I can help with that, too. I don't want you to have to carry all that stuff from the storage locker. You have too many old props and stuff that weigh a ton."

"Into older women?" Trey asked, trying not to laugh. Both of his sons had a crush on Cassidy.

"She's only two years older than me. And I don't have a crush. I was just trying to be helpful." He blushed all the way up to the roots of his dark blond hair, giving away his real intentions.

Trey looked down at his phone. "I'm in charge of green beans. Five gallons of green beans."

His wife squealed suddenly. When Trey looked up she was beaming. "Holt is coming up from Nashville to sing for the party. I'll have both my boys home. But now I need a theme."

"Medieval fair? It should make the Rose sisters remember their childhood."

Taylor glared at her husband. "That's not nice."

"But it's true," Trey chuckled.

"Oh, I have it. Gatsby Glamour with a Southern twist. Think chandeliers and cowboy boots." His wife started muttering to herself as she walked from the room.

Trey followed her into the kitchen. She was already at the table drawing out her vision for the party. He stopped behind her and rested his hands on her shoulders. And when she leaned back against him and smiled at him, he fell in love all over again. Something he did on a daily basis.

Nabi looked out over his small property that connected to Mo and Dani's farm, Desert Sun, from his large porch. His ten-year-old daughter, Faith, was doing something on her computer on the nearby outdoor couch. Ever since she was born, she'd looked up to Kale. He'd shared his love of computers with her.

Nabi's wife, Grace, was sitting next to him reading Gemma's latest book as he pondered his life. He'd just turned fifty, and while he loved his job as head of security for the royal family, he was ready to spend more time with his own family. Since Grace was still teaching kindergarten, she had summers off, and he wanted to spend them with her and Faith.

"Grace," Nabi said, turning to his wife and dropping his voice so Faith wouldn't overhear them. "What do you think about me taking a step back from work?"

A wild curl escaped the headband his wife was wearing and fell across her forehead. "How so?"

"I want to see if I can start working part-time. It will give Nash a chance to run things while I can still train him before handing the whole thing off to him in a couple years."

"Could we go to the lake for a week?" Faith asked as her head remained hidden behind the computer. There was no hiding anything from her.

"I was hoping we could. What do you think, Grace?"

His wife's hand covered his and squeezed. "I think it would be wonderful."

"Did you two know it was the Rose sisters' hundredth birthday?" Faith asked, finally popping up from behind her laptop screen.

"No, when?" Grace asked, turning to look at their daughter while keeping her hand locked with her husband's.

"Day after tomorrow. Kale just texted me. He's coming home for it and said there's this new hack he wants to teach me."

"Should we be letting her do that?" Grace whispered.

Nabi shrugged. "A little late to start pulling her back now. Kale is as smart as they come, so why not let her learn from the best?"

"Make sure you keep an eye on her, though. I don't want Ryan showing up to arrest her one day before school. I'll run inside and grab my phone to see if there is any news about their birthday."

Nabi watched his wife head into the house and took a deep breath. Retirement. Could he do that? The only thing holding him back was knowing he'd grow restless. He wanted to spend time with his family, but he also wasn't the type to sit back and do nothing.

"Oh goodness. We've missed a lot," Grace called out as she pushed open the screen door while looking down at her phone. "We are to bring baked beans and flowers. Dani said I could use our garden or theirs to get them."

"There's a whole field of wildflowers down by the stream at the back of Desert Farm," Faith said excitedly as she closed her laptop.

"Great idea, sweetie. While Dad makes the beans, you and I will pick the flowers."

Nabi sat back and listened to Grace and Faith discussing flowers and decorations. Taylor had written that the theme was Southern Gatsby. He didn't know what the hell that meant, but his wife had squealed with delight. Retirement didn't sound so bad after all . . . As long as he got to keep on beating up bad guys every once in a while.

The Davies Farm was quiet as the evening's warm glow bathed the land around them in oranges and yellows. Marcy sat on her rocking chair, looking out over the land she'd worked since she was eighteen. Her parents had left her to join her brothers in South Carolina after condemning her marriage to Jake. And she'd lost touch with them decades ago. It was something she should mend before time ran out. She'd been busy all these years as a mother to six children, seventeen grandchildren, and no great-grandchildren—yet.

"I think our children think we're getting old," Jake said as he handed her a cup of tea before taking a seat in the rocking chair next to her.

"We *are* getting old," Marcy snickered.

"Well, maybe. But the boys wouldn't let me help mend the fences today."

Marcy reached a hand out and patted her husband's leg. Age has a way of sneaking up on you. It seemed it was just yesterday she had married the love of her life. Now she hardly recognized the age-spotted and wrinkled skin of her own hand. But she recognized the feel of her husband and would until she died.

"You know Betsy and William have decided to move to Florida. We could do that someday."

Jake took off his cowboy hat and set it on the side table next to him. "I would have thought you wanted to see your great-grandchildren running around this place."

"I do. But it won't be that much longer until this house is filled with more family than it can hold."

"It didn't have any trouble holding our boys this afternoon. Don't think I didn't notice the apple pie that was supposed to be my dessert tonight is suddenly gone," Jake smirked.

Marcy smiled at her husband. After all these years, did he really think she forgot about him? "I made two. You have one all to yourself inside."

"I knew there was a reason I married you," Jake teased as he got up and disappeared inside.

Marcy looked back out at the farm that had been in the family for generations. It was time to admit things needed to change. When Jake came back out with a huge slice of pie, Marcy asked him, "What do you think about dividing up the farm to each of the boys? They all have farms that border ours. We can divide it that way."

"Are you really wanting to move, Marcy?" Jake asked, setting his fork down.

Marcy shook her head. "Not yet. We've never really talked about what we want to do with the farm, and I think it would be fair to give a little bit to each son and the house and surrounding couple of acres to Paige."

"I think it's a good idea, but not one I'm ready for. I still enjoy riding through my fields," Jake said, and Marcy had to agree. He still looked handsome as could be sitting on a horse.

"Well, when the time comes, I think we have a plan."

"I'll tell you what my plan is."

Marcy looked over at her husband licking the last crumb from his fork. "What is it?"

"I'm going to get more pie and then kiss you so you know

how much I enjoyed it." Jake sent her a wink and headed back inside.

Marcy heard the screen door slam and in her mind she saw her children running through the same door for dinner, their jeans muddy, their hazel eyes sparkling, and all of them talking at once. It was home. It was her home. Over the years, those children grew into adults. And then it was grandchildren racing through the door for her pies. The door opened and it wasn't an old man she saw. It was Jake, his body lean and muscled, his face filled with a youthful smile, and a slight hint of mischief to his hazel eyes. He leaned over her and kissed her. And for that one moment her arthritis and age spots disappeared, and she was a young girl madly in love with a boy.

6

SIENNA ASHTON PARKER pulled into her driveway and saw the lights in the house begin to flicker. Her dog, Hooch, knew she was home. It had been a long day at the Thoroughbreds' office. She loved her job as a sports psychologist, but it had been a long couple of days with a few of the players facing anxiety over contract negotiations. The summer wasn't a quiet time for the people in the front office.

Sienna pulled into the garage and walked out front to get the mail. The front door opened and Hooch, well over a hundred ten pounds of jowls and rolling muscles, stumbled out the front door. He knocked over a chair as he bounded off the porch and down the driveway.

"There's my baby," Sienna cooed as Hooch tried to slam on the brakes but failed miserably. Instead of stopping, he launched his body upward, slamming two enormous paws into her chest and sending her stumbling backward into the mailbox.

"He's missed you," Ryan called out.

Sienna wedged the small knit baby's cap that had been

left sitting not so innocently in the mailbox onto Hooch's head. "Go see Daddy."

Hooch's deep bark rumbled through Sienna's chest before he turned and ran toward Ryan with the yellow cap barely hanging on as Sienna had stretched it to three times its size in order to fit Hooch's head.

"Another one?" Ryan groaned as he took the knit cap off Hooch.

"She's your mother. You deal with it, or I swear I will tie my tubes."

"Come on now. You know she scares me," Ryan complained, leaning down from the top of the porch to kiss her. "Welcome home. I made dinner."

"Well, I guess that redeems you somewhat from being afraid of your mom," Sienna said, sniffing the air. "Is that—?"

"My homemade gumbo." Ryan smiled.

"You're definitely forgiven." Sienna pushed past him and went straight to the crockpot and sniffed. Her stomach rumbled, and she might have drooled. Living with Hooch was rubbing off on her.

"What do you think about the party for the Rose sisters?" Ryan asked, stirring the gumbo.

"I think they'll find out." Sienna kicked off her heels and took a seat on the barstool.

"We're supposed to bring plates."

"No problem. I'll pick them up tomorrow. Do you want to meet for lunch? I have a break unless someone comes in without an appointment, which is always possible."

Ryan shook his head. "Sorry. I was able to leave early today, but tomorrow we have some training with the DEA office. We're working closely with them on the heroin problem. Apparently they've been having luck using undercover agents."

Sienna licked the spoon Ryan had just used to stir the gumbo. "Haven't you all used undercover work for a long time?"

Ryan shrugged. "They said they're thinking outside the box with people who don't look like agents—like housewives or moms or something. I don't know. They're going to brief us on this new approach tomorrow."

"So you and some PTA moms are going to bring down the heroin dealers? Whatever works. We've upped the number of drug tests for the football team. It's too easy to get and too easy to get hooked on. I'm leading a drug education class next month when the rookies come."

Ryan brought out two bowls and started spooning gumbo into them. "The undercover agents won't be there. We're just learning about different ways to utilize undercover work. But something needs to be done. Four people died last night in one apartment complex from overdosing."

Sienna dug into her gumbo and moaned.

Ryan shook his head with amusement. "I used to be the only one who could get you to make that sound."

"I won't complain if you want to try. I don't want you to lose your touch," Sienna said seductively before ruining the moment by moaning around another mouthful of gumbo.

"My pleasure," Ryan said, scooping his wife up and carrying her down the hall.

"My gumbo!"

Ryan kissed her and gumbo became a distant memory.

~

Deacon McKnight crept through the shadows of the trailer park on the outskirts of Lexington with Detective Andrea Braxton. The trailer park was surrounded by woods and located far enough from town that the criminals who called it home felt safe. Two days before, a fourteen-year-old girl never came home from swimming at the community pool and that investigation led them to the trailer park. The girl's mother and father were frantic. Detective Braxton had recommended the parents hire Deacon to assist her as well since her plate was full of open cases.

Deacon had worked nonstop tracing the girl's footsteps. He'd learned she'd left the pool, and a block away an old lady remembered seeing her pass by as she watered her plants. Two blocks later, Deacon had found a home with a motion-activated smart doorbell. From the far side of the camera, Tisha could be seen walking on the sidewalk, triggering the doorbell to begin recording. She hadn't gotten but three more steps when a rusted-out car approached her and stopped behind her. A man got out, grabbed Tisha, and in seconds had her in the trunk and drove off.

With the tape in hand, Deacon had taken it to Detective Braxton. They visited the elderly neighbor who recognized the car as one of their neighbor's deadbeat sons. It was only a short matter of time before they had the address for the trailer and were hoping to rescue Tisha.

"I'll take the suspect down. You stay here," Detective Braxton whispered as she drew her gun.

Deacon waited as Braxton announced herself and then charged into the trailer. The small bathroom window slid open and the scrawny man from the security footage wiggled out. As he came to his feet, he jumped back in surprise at seeing Deacon.

"Hiya." Deacon smiled as he rammed his fist into the

man's chin, sending him sliding down the side of the trailer. Braxton ran out of the trailer with her arm around Tisha and looked at the unconscious suspect. "He fell trying to get out of the window. Slammed his chin right onto the ground."

Detective Braxton just shook her head and called in the EMTs.

"Tisha," Deacon said, kneeling in front of the tattered and tear-stained girl. Her black braided hair was sticking out in all directions as she clung to the detective. "My name is Deacon McKnight. Your parents, Tyler and Jayla, hired me to find you. Why don't we call them so they know you're safe? Would you like that?"

Tisha nodded her head as Deacon entered the number. "We have her. Hold on."

Tisha grabbed the phone. "Mommy?"

Two hours later, Deacon drove up his long driveway. It was dark, but he had waited until Tisha's parents met her at the hospital before declaring the case closed. The sound of a barking dog reached him as soon as the garage door began rising. Before he could even pull in, the door opened and his wife stood outlined by the kitchen lights.

"Is she safe?" Sydney asked, hurrying down to him as Robyn, their rust-colored vizsla, bounded around carrying a small stuffed toy.

"Yes. Her parents are with her now. The guy thought he could sell her for drugs. Needless to say, he got that idea while high. Then he didn't know what to do with her when he crashed. So he stole money from her backpack and got high again, leaving her tied to the kitchen table."

Deacon kissed his wife and felt centered again. No

matter how many bad things he saw while working, Sydney was his light.

"This probably isn't the right time to tell you that your father sent us something."

Deacon grumbled as he walked inside. "What now?"

"Your old crib." Sydney stepped out of his way to where the crib that had been in the McKnight family for generations stood freshly stained.

"Anything else I should know about?" Deacon asked, collapsing onto the couch.

"Yes, there's a surprise party for the Rose sisters' hundredth birthday in two days. Taylor called me and asked me to make dresses for the ladies to change into once there. It's a Southern Gatsby theme."

"What the hell does that mean?"

Sydney rolled her eyes. "You grew up in Atlanta society and you can't figure that out?"

"What do I need to do?" Deacon asked, trying to not think about all the horrible cotillions he'd been to as a young man.

"Lots and lots of cups. Poppy and Zinnia have been recruited to make a massive amount of Rose sisters' iced tea," Sydney called out as Robyn attacked the toy before grabbing it and running around the living room as fast as she could.

Deacon grasped Sydney's wrist as she walked by and pulled her into his lap. "Sounds like you're going to be busy making dresses. Do you have time with your summer line launching?"

"Syd Inc. is a well-oiled machine. The launch has been great. The review on the clothes has been fantastic. I can afford to take some time off, especially for the Rose sisters."

"I can think of something to do on your time off," Deacon murmured as he ran his lips over her neck.

"Mmm. And what's that?" Sydney asked breathily.

"I think it's about time to get to work on filling that crib."

Mila Ali Rahman swallowed hard as she looked at the pregnancy test. She heard Zain let out a deep ragged breath.

"Negative. Again." Mila's voice came out hoarsely as disappointment strangled her.

"It's okay, sweetheart. We have fun trying, and that's the important part," Zain said, trying to put her at ease.

"No, it's not." Mila struggled to hold back the tears. "Do you have any idea what it's like to have people constantly staring at my stomach? What it's like to have your mom leaving me baby blankets and your dad suggesting baby names? What it's like to have a freaking king ask if you're ovulating? Making a baby should be fun and filled with love. Instead, I'm feeling crushed from the pressure to produce the Prince of Rahmi's heir."

Mila finally felt the levee of tears break. Sobs wracked her body as the pregnancy test fell to the floor. Of course there was a knock at the door at that exact moment. Trembling with emotional exhaustion, Mila pulled away. Zain didn't free her from his grasp.

"Ignore it. You're more important than anything or anyone at the door." Zain brushed back her curly hair and kissed her softly. "Sweetheart, it's only been five months. The doctor warned it could take a while. Don't lose hope."

"But what if I can't—" The doorbell rang.

"I don't care if we can't have a baby. Mila, you're what matters to me."

Mila wanted to believe it. "But the king, the royal line . . ." People thought it was a fairy tale come true to marry a prince. And it was, mostly. But there was also an inordinate amount of pressure and lack of privacy.

"Gabe can handle it. Gosh knows he's getting enough practice," Zain said of his younger-by-a-couple-minutes twin brother.

"Then all hope is lost because the Playboy Prince will never settle down." Mila hiccupped as she laughed.

The doorbell rang again. "Zain! Mila!"

Mila let her head fall back. "Would you see what your mom wants?"

Zain kissed her again. "I'll be right back."

Zain hurried to answer the door. "What, Mom?" He loved his mother. Really, he did. But right now wasn't the best time for her to barge in.

"What took you so long?" she asked hopefully.

"If I don't answer the door, there's a reason."

In that second, his teasing mother saw the look on his face. "What is it?" She grabbed his hand, looking over his body for an injury. "Mila? Is Mila okay?"

Zain paused a heartbeat too long. His mother sucked in a breath. "Mila!"

"Mom," Zain snapped. "Not now."

His mom froze in her steps and took a deep breath. "Is she okay?"

"She's resting now. What did you need so badly that it couldn't wait?"

"Did you know it is the Rose sisters' hundredth birthday?"

"No, I didn't." The Rose sisters were the heart of the

town, but right now Zain was having trouble focusing on anything outside of their home.

"We're having a surprise party at the Ashtons' farm the day after tomorrow. I wanted to ask if you and Mila could supply drinks. Juice for the kids and good stuff for the adults. Oh, and I have something out in the car for you, but it's heavy. Can you get it for me?"

"Sure. I'll be right back."

Dani didn't even wait for the door to close before she ran up the stairs. Her heart sank as she found Mila muffling her cries into a towel on the bathroom floor. Flashbacks of herself on the cold tile floor as she lost her baby hit Dani hard and fast. Without saying a word, she knelt down next to Mila and pulled her close. The negative pregnancy test sat at her feet.

Dani stroked Mila's hair as she heard her son's footsteps pounding up the stairs. He stopped with murder in his eyes as she shooed him out. She knew the look, but she also knew there were some things only another woman could understand. Zain looked pissed, but he took a step back.

"Cry all you want, my dear. It hurts so badly. I know, trust me."

"You don't know!" Mila yelled. Dani remembered the anger well.

"But I do," Dani said softly. "I lost two children from miscarriages. But out of that darkness came the lights of my life. After each miscarriage, I became pregnant. And I know about the pressure, Mila. I know I get carried away thinking of grandchildren, but never think that doesn't mean I don't care about you. I'd rather have you and Zain happy and healthy with no children than have you unhappy and hurt if you can't have them."

"The king—" Mila started, sniffling.

"Can chill. The line will be fine. It just means I'll turn my focus to Gabe for a while," Dani said truthfully. She'd been worried that something was bothering Mila. Dani, of everyone, should have understood it. She felt shame and guilt for the pressure she'd put on her daughter-in-law, even though it was done so good-naturedly. "I won't ask again unless you want me to. And my door is always open if you need to talk."

Mila nodded but still couldn't bring herself to smile. Dani kissed her cheek and motioned for Zain to come back. Zain reached down and picked up his wife and carried her to bed as Dani walked slowly down the stairs.

"I'll be right back," Zain whispered to her.

Zain tucked Mila into bed and followed his mom downstairs. "Right after the party I'm going to take Mila away."

"You're a good husband, Zain. I'm very proud of you. And may I recommend the family house in the Bahamas? I'll make sure no one bothers you while you're there. And I'm so sorry. I shouldn't have put that pressure on you. I, of all people, should have known better."

"I know it was out of love, Mom."

"It doesn't matter. Just remember, your father and I are here if you need anything. See you at the party, son, and only if you two feel like it."

Zain kissed his mother's cheek and pulled out his phone. A couple weeks on the family's private island sounded like the perfect escape.

7

MATT WALZ LOOKED down at the sparkling women rolling on the ground. So this is what being a small-town sheriff was like. He took a deep breath and jumped into the fray of the Miss Keeneston beauty pageant. Apparently the runner-up thought the winner had cheated and didn't deserve to ride on the Fourth of July float next month.

"Son of a—" Matt yelled as one of them bit his ankle. "Ella! Don't make me tell your mother!"

The girl in blue sequins looked up at him as she tried to rip the crown from the winner's head. "She's right there, Sheriff."

Matt let his head fall back for just a moment as he tried to regain control on his patience. His walkie-talkie went off as his deputy, Cody Gray, called him. "What is it, Gray? I have my hands full."

"I just got a text about the surprise party for the Rose sisters' hundredth birthday, but when I pulled their licenses it says they're eighty-three. Do I need to do something about that?"

Ella stopped ripping the crown from the winner's head. "It's the Rose sisters' birthday?"

The winner's head popped up. "Ah, congratulations on your win, Mary Ellen," Matt said, hoping that didn't restart the fight.

"Thanks. But did he say surprise party?"

Matt told Cody not to worry about enforcing the correct age on their license since they didn't drive anymore and pulled out his phone as the pageant girls untangled themselves.

"We have to do something special for the Rose sisters," Mary Ellen told the group as they clustered around their new leader. "Ella, do you think you could make a huge batch of your delicious beer cheese?"

"You bet," Ella said, adjusting her evening gown to cover an exposed breast.

"I can make Benedictine finger sandwiches," someone called out.

As Matt quietly slipped from the pageant, the girls all had their cell phones out and were bombarding Kenna, Dani, and Paige with texts. After all, that's who sent him and his wife, Riley, the request to bring the disposable silverware.

Riley Davies Walz was working on her laptop when her husband came home. He took off his gun belt and laid it on the bar top before coming over to give her a kiss. Riley set aside her computer as he took a seat next to her on the couch. He tugged at several strands of red hair from the knot she'd tied it in at the beginning of the day.

"Busy day at the farm?" Matt asked, taking in her dust-smudged face.

"Yes. Dad was with his brothers mending fences over at Grandma and Grandpa's farm today so I helped move all the cattle to the new pasture. And now this," she waved to the computer.

Matt groaned. "Please tell me your father hasn't sent another castration video. Does he really think we don't have sex?" Her father, Cy, was a little . . . well, he was just her dad and slightly overprotective. Her mother, Gemma, on the other hand was trying everything she could think of to hurry along children for them.

"No. It's about my term in the state legislature. I finished my second term so I have to run for reelection in November," Riley explained.

"I thought you wanted to run for reelection." Matt said, pulling her legs over his lap so he could hold her closer.

"I do. But Reagan has been disappearing a lot when she's not flying horses to different farms and racetracks. Then Dad has been stretched thin, trying to care for our farm plus his parents'. I worry about not having the time to help out when they need it. I work the farm nine months of the year, but if Reagan disappears and Dad gets busy at the other farm, who will take care of our farm?" Riley let out a sigh and Matt pulled her closer.

"Riley, the better question is who will look out for the people of Keeneston if you aren't in office? You've helped with farming legislation this year. You stopped the corruption that threatened the town last year. You know there's more work to be done and you know you have ideas on how to do it," Matt said gently. "And you know I'll help out on the farm as much as I can. Even if your father threatens me every time your mother mentions grandchildren."

That was the same argument Riley made to herself and why she'd already filled out the form she needed to file to declare her candidacy. All she had to do was send it, something she would do first thing in the morning. She had her big family to lean on. She knew if her dad needed help and she couldn't be there, the Davies family would step up and help. Hearing Matt's encouraging words was all she needed to solidify the decision.

"My dad won't actually shoot the father of my children," Riley said as she tried to sound convincing.

Matt scooped her up into his arms and carried her down the hall. "Let's find out."

Riley laughed as she threw her arms around her husband's neck. "The bed is that way."

"The warm-up is in the shower. I have so much sparkling shit on me from breaking up a fight at the pageant I'm afraid to see what happens if I sneeze."

"Aw, did the big bad beauty queens scare you?" Riley asked sympathetically.

"Yes." Matt set her down and turned on the water. "It was horrible. Clouds of hairspray," Matt complained as he stripped her shirt from her body. "And the tape! Don't get me started on the tape they put on their bodies. It was stronger than duct tape. That's just not normal." Matt reached down and pulled off Riley's jeans. "And then Ella bit me!"

Riley laughed as her husband quickly shed his clothes. "She did not."

"She did! Right on my ankle." Matt showed her as they stepped into the large tiled shower with two showerheads and a bench.

"My poor husband," Riley said, directing him to sit on

the bench. "Let's see what I can do about making you feel better."

Nash and Sophie Dagher basked nude on their private beach in the Maldives. Just twelve days before, she had been Sophie Davies and now she was a married woman. Tomorrow morning, she and Nash would return to the real world. Their honeymoon had been everything they could have dreamed—peaceful and solitary. No phones, no one shooting at them, no one gossiping or placing bets on them. Just she and her husband.

"Shall we go for a quick snorkel before we get ready for dinner?" Nash asked. She felt the rumble of his words as she ran her hand absently over his chest.

"Hmm. Get ready for dinner? Nash, it's only two o'clock."

Nash ran a hand down her back, over her hip, and up to cup her breast. "I have plans that may delay your getting dressed."

"Are you sure we have to go back?" Sophie asked as Nash laid her in the sand and covered her body with his.

"Shall we extend the honeymoon, wife?" Nash bent his head to her sun-kissed breasts and swirled his tongue around her peaked nipples.

"Definitely."

They had been late to dinner and Nash couldn't wipe the grin from his face because of it. They were staying in a private beachside villa at the end of the small resort. They had snorkeled, scuba dived, and boated around the beautiful islands while enjoying plenty of time basking in the sun and in each other.

The open-air luxury restaurant seated them at their romantic waterside table. Nash scanned the menu, but even the complete relaxation of their honeymoon didn't stop him from noticing the hushed, yet heated, discussion between the maître d' and a person from hotel services.

"Is there a problem?" Sophie asked, not even taking her eyes from the menu.

Nash saw the man from hotel services gesture toward them. "I think we're being discussed."

"I think I'll have the sea bass. Why don't you see what they want? It could have to do with our leaving tomorrow."

Nash slowly raised his hand and with the curl of his fingers gestured for the two men to come to them. The maître d' stopped first. "I am sorry for the interruption, Mr. and Mrs. Dagher. I know you said not to be bothered while on your honeymoon, but it appears you've a message from Kingston . . . Kenston?"

"Keeneston. It's okay. I'll take it." Nash held out his hand and took the note from the hotel employee as Sophie tipped them. The men hurried from the table arguing as Nash read the note. "It appears we will be arriving right in time for the Rose sisters' surprise hundredth birthday party. Dani says not to worry about a thing, just show up at the Ashton Farm at six o'clock."

"We get into Lexington at five-thirty," Sophie told him. "It'll be tight to get there on time, but I think we can. Especially if I drive."

"I think your love for speed is well documented, Soph. You almost sent me careening from the boat."

Sophie giggled and Nash laughed. He raised his glass to his wife. "To the Rose sisters and to my wife."

"To my husband."

"And to our future children."

They clinked glasses as the sun began to set over the crystal-blue ocean.

8

KENNA STOOD like a general commanding an army as the people of Keeneston flooded into the Ashton Farm. The football team raised the tent and then carried in tables. Her friends were unloading the decorations from the trailer Taylor Everett had brought. The Belles, the town's supposed charitable organization for unmarried women, but really more like a husband hunters club, sat with Grace and her daughter, Faith, separating wildflowers into cowboy boots for centerpieces.

"What do you need us to do now?" Paige and Dani asked as they wiped dirty hands on their jeans.

Kenna looked at her watch. "Crap. It's noon!"

"Don't worry. We'll have plenty of time to get this finished," Paige reassured her.

"No, not that. Everything is perfect here, but *everyone* is here!" Kenna waved her arm frantically at the entire backyard filled with people.

"Oh, crap!" Dani gasped. "No one is at the café!"

"Shit," Paige said under her breath. "Grace, Faith, Knox, Nikki!" Paige yelled.

Nikki's gigantic boobs poked up first. Then Knox set down the mallet he was using to hammer in the tent stakes as Grace and Faith extricated themselves from all the wildflowers and cowboy boots. "You all need to grab a couple of people and head to the café. There's no one there!" Paige called out.

Nikki, as president of the Belles, was feared and loathed but wielded too much power to be denied. She reached for the nearest Belle who screeched in surprise as Nikki's talons sunk into her arm before dragging her off. Grace and Faith hurried off, picking up Addison Rooney and Ava Miller, both of whom had babysat Faith before. Addison was the daughter of the town's two defense attorneys, Henry and Neely Grace, and a lawyer in her own right. Ava was in medical school in Lexington where her mother, Emma, was also a doctor. Her father was the retired deputy everyone called Noodle for his love of noodling catfish.

"Couldn't you have sent someone else beside Knox?" Aniyah huffed as she stood nearby with a small battery-operated fan.

"Why?" Kenna asked.

"I was enjoying the view of that fine specimen." Aniyah pouted as Knox slipped a shirt on over his head, covering his rippled abs, and grabbed a couple of his buddies to go to the café.

"And what would DeAndre say?" Dani teased.

"My Sugarbear knows where my heart lies. I was simply appreciating God's fine work," Aniyah said, turning her fan back on.

Kenna looked to where Aniyah's state trooper boyfriend stood, talking to Knox before he jumped into the waiting truck. DeAndre nodded and walked toward the tent. He stripped off his shirt and picked the mallet back up as Dani, Kenna, and Paige sucked in a breath.

Dani snatched Aniyah's fan from her and blasted her and her friends. "What do you think you're doing?" Aniyah squawked.

"Observing God's artwork," Kenna replied without taking her eyes from DeAndre's dark, rippled body.

"He's younger than our son."

"Son of a—" Kenna jumped as Dani and Paige let out a squeak.

Will crossed his arms over his chest and tried not to grin. "Busted."

Kenna rolled her eyes. "I'll have Nikki take off her top when she gets back so we'll be even."

Will shuddered. "What are you trying to do? Give me nightmares?" He leaned forward and placed his lips by her ear. "I can think of something you could do to make it up to me."

Kenna felt her lips tugging into a smile as she shook her head. Her husband was incorrigible.

"The guys are here to help. The cows are at the butcher and will be ready tonight. We'll start smoking some of the meat then so I may not be home until real late. So, what do you need us to do?" Will asked her.

Kenna welcomed her friends and within minutes they were fanning out over the backyard. The tent was finished, the tables were rolling in, chairs were being set up, and the table of honor was being raised.

Miss Lily Rae Rose sat with her sisters, Daisy Mae and Violet Fae, at the Blossom Café. Their very distant and young cousins, Poppy and Zinnia, were waiting on the few occupied tables. Lily's eyes narrowed.

"Something is going on," she told her sisters as Nikki Canter and one of the nameless blonde Belles hurried into the café.

"Why do you say that, Lil?" Daisy asked as she took a sip of her iced tea.

"Look around. None of the regulars are here and Knox just slid his truck to a stop outside so fast there's still smoke in the air," Lily said as her sisters looked up to see Knox and some of his teammates stumble through the café door.

"Hi, Miss Lily, Miss Daisy, Miss Violet," the boys said politely as they took a seat at a nearby table.

"Hello, boys. What has you all in a lather?" Miss Lily asked, putting on her best innocent old lady face.

"Just taking a quick lunch break before getting back to the farm. Helping Coach Ashton out before I leave for college. He's been telling us he got in great shape by tossing hay." Knox snorted in disbelief before shrugging it off. "So, we're giving it a try."

"That's nice, dear," Miss Lily smiled before turning back to her sister. "That young man's pants are about to burst into flames for all the lying he's doing."

"Lily Rae," Violet scolded, shaking her white head at her sister. "You know darn well Will did such a thing. Nothing strange is going on."

The door opened again as Addison, Ava, Faith, and Grace came in laughing. Lily looked to her sisters and simply raised an eyebrow as Addison and Ava sat at one table and Faith and Grace at the table next to them.

"Okay, so it's a little strange," Daisy agreed as the newly arrived all shouted out their hellos the to them.

"I'm telling you, something is up," Miss Lily promised as

she turned up her hearing aid. She'd find out what it was if it was the last thing she did.

Ten minutes later, the door opened again and Nora Owens, the owner of the Fluff and Buff, walked in. She wore all black to make the salon look fancier. Her blonde hair was cut in a short chin-length bob and highlighted with pink and purple streaks.

Violet leaned over to her sisters. "I'd love to have purple hair."

"When you're as old as we are, there's no point in waiting," Daisy snorted as they watched Nora pick up a to-go order and head their way.

"Hi, ladies. I'll see you tomorrow for your perms," Nora smiled as she stopped at the table.

"I want purple hair," Violet told her.

Nora blinked once and then nodded. "I can do that."

"I want yellow. Not like a canary. I don't want to look like a bird," Daisy said, getting into it, too.

"I can do a blonde on you that will look pale yellow," Nora told her.

"Come in, Lily. Do something, too. You're always such a stick in the mud," Violet taunted.

"Hey, I'm the one who took us skydiving," Lily protested. But as she looked at Nora's youthful hair, she knew she wanted to do something fun, too. "Pink! I want a light pink like you have."

The sisters giggled and Nora's smiled widened. "It'll be so much fun. Can you get there an hour earlier, though?"

"We'll see you then," Lily told her, getting into the idea of doing something radical for their birthday. Then she froze as Nora left. She leaned forward. "I got it! They're doing something for our birthday."

"Which one is it?" Violet asked. "I've lied about my age so much I don't remember how old I am."

The three sisters thought for a moment. "Well, it doesn't matter," Lily said. "That's why they're being strange. Let's see what Aniyah says about us changing up the schedule for tomorrow."

Lily dialed Aniyah and waited for her to answer. "Yes?" Aniyah asked, sounding distracted.

"She's distracted," Lily whispered to her sisters. "It's Lily. I was hoping you wouldn't mind a change of plans tomorrow."

"Sure thing, Miss Lily. What's up?"

"Do you have a moment? I don't want to interrupt anything."

"Girl, you aren't interrupting anything. I'm over here watching Will Ashton work the football players at his farm. It's a mix of the seniors who just graduated and some of his pro players. Half of them have their shirts off and—"

Daisy shook her head. "See, nothing. You're imagining things, Lil."

Lily's doubts remained as she relayed the change of times for the next day. Aniyah was nice enough to drive them around to their appointments when she wasn't working in Frankfort as Riley Davies Walz's assistant. Aniyah was only in Frankfort part-time now that the session had ended.

"See, I told you they weren't up to anything," Daisy scolded when Lily got off the phone.

"*Hmph.*" Lily would just see about that.

The tables were up, and it was time to decorate. The men were running the electric work for the chandeliers as the women began decorating the tables. As soon as this was done, they'd head back to Keeneson High School to make another round of desserts. After baking half of them that morning, they had needed a break. This was their break.

"We've got a problem!" Aniyah yelled as she ran toward them on her tiptoes to prevent her five-inch heels from sinking into the grass. "The Rose sisters think something is up. They changed their plans for tomorrow, and Miss Lily sounded real suspicious."

"What did you tell them?" Kenna asked a little more harshly than she meant to.

"I told them we were at Will's farm watching some of his players tossing hay. Will suggested it to us earlier in case something came up."

Kenna looked frantically around. "Sienna!"

"Yes, Mom?" Sienna asked as she smoothed a wrinkle from a tablecloth.

"Which Thoroughbred players live nearby?"

"Jaylen King moved to a house about twenty minutes away and Zack Sanders is about fifteen minutes away. Why?" Sienna told them as she walked closer.

"Will! Trey! Get over here now!" Kenna yelled to her husband teetering on a ladder and the man holding the ladder.

"What's going on?" Sienna asked again.

"Miss Lily called Aniyah." Kenna relayed as Will and Trey joined them.

Trey looked down at his phone. "Definitely suspicious. Knox just texted. They asked him where on the farm he was working out. Luckily he remembered the lie and told Miss Lily the same thing."

"Call the players and get all the seniors and the recent grads over to the barn now! Trey and Sienna, get as many players as possible there as well! Hurry!" Kenna screamed.

People scattered quickly. Boys leapt into the back of pickup trucks. Men and women jumped into their cars and drove them into every nearby barn they could fit them in before closing the doors. Kenna stood outside staring at the main house from the drive and sighed in relief. Nothing was visible from the road as very expensive sports cars and trucks raced past her. The NFL players had arrived.

9

ANIYAH HELD up a hose and sprayed the players down as some stripped their shirts off. She grabbed some hay and rubbed their muscled bodies with it. Lordy, the best thing she ever did was move to Keeneston. Goodness knows she loved her man, too. DeAndre was sitting at a supposed speed trap to let them know when the Rose sisters were getting near.

Aniyah picked up some hay and slathered Jaylen King, the star running back. Even in her five-inch heels, she only reached his chest. He sent her a wink and moved on to tossing hay with the rest of the hosed-down and hayed-covered players.

Deon Wofford, Zack Sanders, and Adrian Hummel filed in and waited for Aniyah to dirty them up.

Five minutes was the text Aniyah got from DeAndre that really sent them scrambling. "They're almost here!"

Will and Trey got the players in line as some jumped on the bales of hay and others tossed the heavy bales weighing eighty pounds or more. Aniyah hurried as she turned off the hose, rolled it up, and took a seat on the swing on Will's back porch. She flipped on her fan, hid her dirty shoes under herself, and waited for the Rose sisters.

Minutes later, the three old ladies rounded the house with trays in hand. Clever girls. Aniyah almost applauded them. Instead, she waved them over. "Did you bring me lunch?"

"No. Knox made it sound like a hard workout. He was waiting on some to-go orders when we left. We thought the men would like some cookies so we had Poppy drive us out here," Miss Lily said, not once looking at Aniyah. Instead she scanned the entire area.

"Well, I'll take one. It's hard work watching them."

"Oh my!" Miss Violet gasped as Zach, the six-foot-five mountain of a man, lifted a hay bale over his head and threw it a shocking distance with a grunt.

Zack heard her and turned to see the trio of old ladies. "Well, if it isn't the Thoroughbreds' best fans. Did you bring us something to eat?" Zack was already looking at the trays they held as he jogged over toward them.

"Oh my," Miss Lily whispered a moment before the lineman wrapped all three sisters into a giant hug.

"Hey, guys," Zack shouted. "The Rose sisters brought cookies."

Bales of hay were dropped as the men thundered toward the Rose sisters.

Ten minutes later, the trays were empty and Will and Trey were yelling for the men to get back to work. Miss Lily stared at them, lifting, tossing, and jumping various-sized bales of hay.

"See? Nothing." Daisy crossed her arms over her chest and stared her sister down. "Now can we go? Charlie wants to watch some movie with me tonight and now I need a shower. I don't want to explain why I smell like sweaty man."

Violet sighed. "Wasn't that great? I can say I had the NFL's best running back in my arms."

Lily did smile at that. "You mean you suffocated the NFL's best running back in your sagging bosom."

"You say tomato, I say who cares? I had him in my arms," Violet smirked back as she sent the young Jaylen a wink. "Come on, Lil. Let's go. We need our beauty rest. Anton is going to cook us all dinner tomorrow and Zinnia said she's baking us a cake."

"I guess you're right." Lily said as they waved goodbye to the players.

"See you tomorrow, ladies!" Aniyah called after them as they slowly made their way to the car they'd made Poppy drive them in.

Poppy was talking to Kenna as they approached. "Hello, dear," Miss Lily called out.

Kenna turned and smiled at them. She kissed each cheek and wished them a happy early birthday. It was hard to believe little Kenna Mason wasn't from Keeneston. It had been a hard decision when the Roses had stepped back from matchmaking, but leaving it in the hands of Kenna, Dani, and Paige was the best decision the sisters could have made. Bless their hearts, they couldn't match anyone up to save their lives, but Lily and her sisters sure did have fun watching them try. "Who's up next?"

Kenna didn't even pretend to not know what she was talking about. "Gabe. Dani is set on stopping his wandering ways."

"What's the plan?" Daisy asked.

"There's going to be a charity ball. Dani has invited the

best of the best eligible women to attend. All bride material."

"Very good. Poppy, dear, we need to get home. Will we see you tomorrow, Kenna?" Lily asked as they started to get into the car.

"Probably," Kenna smiled. "But if I don't, have a very happy birthday." Kenna leaned into the car and kissed Lily's cheek before going to the back and doing the same with her sisters.

"Happy birthday!" Kenna called out as Poppy drove them away. Maybe her sisters were right. Nothing strange going on at all, but she'd ask her husband anyway. John always knew what was going on and he was on even more of a mission now that DeAndre Drews was finding out gossip quicker. Yes, her husband would know for sure.

"I don't know, Lily Rae. I haven't heard anything."

"You stubborn billy goat! Tell me right now if you know anything about something going on for our birthday."

John shrugged his shoulders. "Really, Lil. I haven't heard anything besides what we husbands have planned and you know about that."

"Fine. Maybe nothing is going on."

"Well, I wouldn't say that. I heard all about Violet smothering Jaylen King in her boobs."

"You can hear that, but you can't hear if Kenna or that group has anything planned for our birthday?" Miss Lily shook her head.

"Do you want something big for your birthday? I know it's a big one for us this year." John was one of the people who knew how old she really was because he'd gone to high school with her. Earlier that year, she'd thrown him a party as well but hadn't thought to make it a large one. It had just been with her sisters and their husbands. When you reached the age they had, birthday parties just seemed childish . . . and maybe that's why Lily wanted one. She wanted to feel young again.

"No. I'm sorry. I guess old age just snuck up on me. I am going to dye my hair pink tomorrow, though."

John chuckled as he rested his hand on her leg. "You'll look beautiful with pink hair, Lil."

Lily laid her head on his shoulder as they looked out over the backyard. "I love you, John. You're my best gift."

"I love you, too, Lil."

The sky had turned to night long ago but the women were still baking in the school cafeteria. Their husbands had brought them dinner and they'd talked about what was left to do before heading out to the farm to check on the Davies brothers smoking the meat. Some of the younger kids would spend the night there keeping an eye on the four large smokers.

The buzzer went off and Paige pumped her fist in the air. "Done!" She pulled the last tray of BLT bites stuffed inside cherry tomatoes from the oven. "They'll just have to be reheated for a couple seconds tomorrow."

Annie groaned. "I have ten more minutes on my last apple pies and I'm about to fall asleep."

"You can help me decorate these cupcakes," Katelyn suggested as she stretched out her fingers. "Three dozen to go."

"You don't want me doing that. I'm not good at making

pretty things," Annie told her, stepping away from the bag of icing Katelyn held out.

"I'll help. I love frosting things," Tammy said. "And I finished my cookies thirty minutes ago."

Tammy grabbed the bag of icing and began topping off the cupcakes with delicate swirls in between shooting some the icing into her mouth.

"I love icing so much," she told the group who was staring at her through a mouthful of light purple icing. The cupcakes were in yellow, purple, and pink, the Roses' favorite colors.

The buzzer sounded again. "Thank goodness. My last brownies," Morgan groaned with pleasure as she pulled the last two trays from another oven.

"I'm so happy the pageant girls are helping with the food. I was afraid I'd have to make more appetizers," Paige said with relief as she went to clean up.

Kenna looked down at her list. "When we all finish up here we are done for the night!"

The women gave as much of a cheer as they could. They were tired, their feet ached, and their fingers hurt. They just wanted to sleep.

"I've never made so much potato salad in my life," Gemma said, putting a cover over the last batch of salad and dragging it to the walk-in refrigerator.

"What is left for tomorrow?" Tammy asked before squeezing some more frosting into her mouth.

"The kids will bring their things over in the morning. So we just need to set out the plates, silverware, napkins, and get the coolers filled with the drinks. Poppy said that the Rose sisters have no idea what's going on. They were suspicious but have no evidence. Zinnia is making a birthday cake for them for their dinner with their husbands, whom we will fill in on the plan as soon as Aniyah drops the Roses off at the Fluff and Buff. But Zinnia said she'll make a real fancy ceremonial cake for the birthday girls to cut and eat from while everyone else can snack on these amazing-smelling desserts." Kenna looked back down at her list.

"I think that's all. We need to be visible in town tomorrow," Kenna told them. "Aniyah said she's taking the sisters to the hair salon at three. From three to six, we will all be at Ashton Farm touching up decorations and setting out food. The town is arriving at Dani's farm at five. Then a bunch of the boys will be shuttling them across the pasture that backs up to the Ashton Farm and up to the tent so that no cars or people will be visible from the street if they drive by for any reason. Or when Aniyah brings them up to the house."

The buzzer beeped again and Annie leapt up. "Done!" She set the pies on the cooling rack and turned off the oven.

Kenna looked around the kitchen and nodded to herself. "Okay, let's get to bed. Tomorrow's the big day."

10

Aniyah pulled to a stop in front of the Fluff and Buff. The door was open and the sound of chatter flowed out of the small salon. Aniyah helped the ladies from the car as people walked by wishing them a happy birthday.

Three Belles sat with their nails under a fan as they chatted. "Happy Birthday," they sang out simultaneously to the Rose sisters.

Aniyah took a peek at their nails. "Oooh, I like that color," she said, looking at the hot pink. "When I get back, can you do that color on me?"

"You're leaving?" Miss Lily asked, still suspicious.

"Let it go, Lil. Nothing is going on," Daisy harrumphed.

"Yeah, Aniyah told us the other day she was going to run some errands and then come back for us." Violet turned away from her sister and picked up a lilac-colored nail polish. "Can you make my hair this color?"

Nora smiled widely. "This is going to be so much fun. Come on, ladies, let's pick out your new look."

"Call me if you need anything. I'll be back in a little

while." Aniyah waved goodbye and headed out the door. She drove out of sight before calling Kenna. "It's a go."

As Aniyah made her way out to the farm, a steady stream of vehicles filled in around her. She parked in the back of Desert Sun Farm and saw a few of the football players from the day before driving passenger ATVs with room for six people on them.

"Aniyah!"

Aniyah turned around as she closed her door and saw Layne, Reagan, Piper, and Carter walking toward her with their hands filled with various items.

"Do y'all need any help?"

"Nope," Carter replied. "We've got it. Our parents called and sent us to get more stuff. Everyone is arriving now to help out while some of us will drive through downtown every now and then so it doesn't appear empty."

Aniyah slid into the seat next to Reagan. "Hey, girl. I haven't seen you around much."

Reagan smiled, making the freckles across her nose scrunch slightly. "Yeah, you get stuck with the bad twin."

Aniyah laughed. "Riley isn't so bad now that no one is trying to kill her. But can you believe the Capitol Police took my gun away? Shoot one little toe . . ."

"Somehow I don't think that stops you," Carter said from the back bench of the ATV.

Aniyah didn't bother replying since he was right. Instead, she just winked as they drove through a gate connecting the two farms. As they drove over the gently rolling hills of the large pastures, the back of William and Betsy's house came into view. A giant white tent covered the backyard. Betsy's flower garden lined the front of the tent, creating pops of reds, oranges, yellows, and purples.

The ATV pulled to a stop and Aniyah watched in awe as

Kenna stood like a conductor moving people as if they were music notes in the air. The ATV emptied out and soon enough another appeared with Matt and Riley, Zain and Mila, and Deacon and Sydney all holding mountains of items.

Sydney blinked her eyes open. She'd been up for too many hours straight to even count. But in her hands were three gorgeous dresses with a little country and a lot of glam. "Are Ryan and Sienna here?" Sydney asked the couples in the ATV with her.

"Nope. They're on downtown duty," Zain answered as he kept one hand on Mila and the other on the stack of five crates of drinks that reached almost to the roof of the ATV.

Deacon hopped out as people swarmed them to help unload. For just a minute, Zain finally left Mila's side and Sydney approached her. "Are you okay? Zain is hovering more than usual."

The area under Mila's eyes was so dark even the heavy amount of concealer she used couldn't hide it. The lines around her eyes and mouth were strained as well and the smile she was giving was anything but real.

"Fine. Just haven't been sleeping well."

Sydney reached out and took her friend's hand. "Deacon's investigative skills are wearing off on me. I know it's more than that, but if you don't want to talk about it, that's okay. Just know I'm always here to distract you if you want or to talk if you want."

"Thank you," Mila said, squeezing her hand. "I don't want to talk about it now, but soon. Zain and I are going away for a couple of weeks to relax. We'll leave tomorrow if not sooner."

"How nice. Deacon and I should do that."

"Do what?" Deacon asked after having set down the massive box of plastic cups.

"Go on vacation," Sydney told him. "Zain and Mila leave tomorrow for a couple weeks."

"That does sound like a good idea. As soon as you finish with the launch we can start planning."

Deacon took the dresses from her and headed into the house to the room Betsy had put aside for the Rose sisters to change into, and Sydney headed into the tent.

Taylor had three massive chandeliers dripping with crystals hanging from the top of the tent. Streamers entwined with strands of white lights hung from the middle of the tent to the side along the entire length of it. Bouquets of gold, silver, and black balloons bracketed the food tables and the raised table where the Rose sisters would sit near the back of the tent. It was as beautiful as the guests of honor themselves.

"Grandma, Grandpa!" Carter called out happily as he set down his items. William and Betsy Ashton sat happily at a table surrounded by friends and family.

"There's my boy," Grandma Betsy said with a twinkle in her eye. Carter leaned down so she could kiss his cheek—something she'd done every time she'd seen him since he was born.

"Are you ready for one last party before you leave for Florida?" Carter asked, kneeling before his elderly grandparents. His grandfather had been just like Carter's father, but over the last couple of years he suddenly appeared old. It was hard for both Carter and Will to see since Grandpa William had always seemed invincible.

"We sure are, dear," Betsy said, taking her husband's hand. "Is there a special young lady you're bringing tonight, Carter?"

"Betsy, leave the young man alone," William chuckled.

"Young? He's thirty years old!"

"I'm practically ancient," Carter teased.

"Ah, there're my dear friends. Hello, Carter. How's the farm?" Marcy Davies asked as she walked to the table. Jake held out the chair next to Betsy for her and then moved to sit next to William.

"It's good. Thank you, Mrs. Davies. I have some two-year-olds I'm hoping to take to the Derby next year." Carter leaned forward and kissed his grandparents' cheeks. "I'll let y'all talk. Don't get into trouble. I've heard stories of what happens when the four of you get together."

Betsy watched her grandson walk off and shook her head. "He needs a wife."

"Don't they all?" Marcy laughed to her best friend.

"And children. We need great-grandchildren."

"You're preaching to the choir, Betsy," Marcy said, taking in her children and grandchildren working around the tent.

Betsy watched Kenna hand off a clipboard to Veronica Pritchard, Zain's right-hand gal for diplomatic issues. There was probably nothing the blonde knockout couldn't handle. She was in a sheath sundress and flats, which was a casual look for her. Her hair was pulled back into a ponytail, but her lips were still bright red.

"Too bad she's a lesbian," Betsy muttered. "She and Carter would look amazing together."

"Isn't that always the case?" Marcy asked. "Remember that man we met when our husbands were overseas?"

"Oh, the Spanish man?" Betsy giggled as if she were twenty again.

"*Hola*. I hope you don't mind I'm not wearing a shirt," Marcy tried to imitate the deep, accented voice.

"And we just stared at all those muscles," Betsy said as she and Marcy had to start fanning themselves even after so many decades.

"And then we met his boyfriend," Marcy said as they both broke out in laughter.

"What are you two laughing about?" William asked, causing the women to laugh even harder.

"Just an old memory, dear," Betsy answered as they broke into a fresh round of giggles.

Betsy looked up as the volume in the tent rose. A young man in white T-shirt, jeans, and a dark brown cowboy hat had just arrived holding a guitar case. "Holt is here from Nashville! It will be a treat to hear him play. I hear he's making quite the name for himself down there."

"Taylor said he's starting his junior year at college there, too. I don't know how he has time to do both."

"Oh my," Betsy said, fanning herself again. "I swear, that man just gets better with age." She watched as Ahmed walked in. His muscles still strained against his black T-shirt and the few silver strands of hair that dared peek out of his temples only made him more sinfully handsome.

The women giggled again as the men next to them chuckled at whatever they were talking about. These were the happy memories Betsy was going to take with her. The friendship, the love, and her family. She was very blessed indeed.

~

It was perfect. Kenna and Will had driven around Keeneston and even walked past the window of the Fluff and Buff. But now it was five and a steady stream of people were arriving.

The food tables were all laid out. The tables were decorated. The lights twinkled as much as the sequins on the women's Gatsby-inspired dresses. It was the crucial time to get everyone gathered. Aniyah had left to delay the Rose sisters, who had to be nearing the completion of their hair styling. She would text as soon as they were on their way.

Paige would be going down now with a beach hat that needed to be delivered to Betsy before they left for Florida. She had enough practice convincing her brothers to do things by making them think it was their idea to get the Rose sisters to suggest that they take it to Betsy. And ten minutes later when Aniyah texted that the game was in play, Kenna knew the Rose sisters had taken the bait.

"Thirty minutes to go!" Kenna said into Holt's microphone. The full tent cheered, and Kenna looked down at a fully checked list. She had done it.

11

MISS LILY STARED at herself in the mirror. Her hair was pink. Not a bright neon pink that made you laugh out loud, but a pretty whisper of a pink that made someone do a double take to make sure they weren't hallucinating.

"Oh, Lil. That looks beautiful on you."

Lily turned to see her sisters standing to the side of the mirror. Tall, stiff Daisy was vibrant as a yellow blonde. Mischievous and slightly wild Violet looked cool and edgy with her light purple hair.

"It's amethyst. Isn't it pretty?" Violet asked, doing a slow spin.

"It's you," Miss Lily whispered, reaching her hands out to her sisters. "It's us."

She felt silly getting misty-eyed. They'd been through heartbreak, losing their parents, running businesses, playing matchmaker, granting wishes, and then finding love again together. And now they were turning . . . well, a year older. And at their age, every year was one that should be celebrated.

"We might look like Easter eggs when we're all standing

together," Daisy teased as they stepped to Lily's side and looked into the mirror.

Aniyah clasped her freshly polished hands together. "You ladies are a vision. It makes my heart smile just seeing you."

Lily looked at the hatbox and then back at Aniyah. "Maybe we should run home to show the men before we deliver the hat?"

Aniyah shrugged. "Whatever you want. I'm at your driving disposal for the next hour, but then me and my Sugarbear have special plans." Aniyah winked and Lily knew exactly what Aniyah meant. After all, she'd seen DeAndre without his shirt on when he was helping rehang a couple of shutters at the breakfast for them. Lily might be old, but she wasn't dead.

With a sigh, Lily had to admit she'd been wrong. John would tease her for it, but Lily really thought the town was up to something for their birthday. "No, that's all right. I want to make sure I see Betsy and William before they leave."

"Right this way, ladies."

Lily followed Aniyah out to her car and sat in the back with Violet as Daisy took the front passenger seat. The ride out to the Ashton Farm was always beautiful. The grass was green, the weather warm, and the horses frisky. It was what made Keeneston so special.

Lily watched the large white-brick house of William and Betsy's draw nearer as they drove up the long driveway lined on both sides with pastures full of horses. Aniyah stopped at the front door and Lily pushed the door open. It was hard to think about this great house without William and Betsy in it. Will and Kenna would make it their own, but it would always be Betsy's house. At least in her mind.

Aniyah retrieved the hatbox from the trunk before they slowly made their way up the stairs to the large rectangular brick patio. Aniyah rang the bell for them and chatted on about something. Lily had to admit she had tuned out after leaving the salon. For some reason, her mind was on the past—all those decades ago when William and Betsy were just high schoolers along with Jake and Marcy. In Lily's mind, that was just a few years ago. Her mind hadn't caught up with the fact that her body was as old as it was. She wouldn't even think the actual number.

The door opened and William smiled out to them. Lily shook off her melancholy and smiled warmly up at him. "We have a delivery for your wife."

William looked down at the hatbox Aniyah was holding and nodded. "Apparently Betsy must have a beach hat and none would do except for one made by Paige. A little bit of home to take with us on our new adventure. Come on in. Betsy is on the back patio."

Lily and her sisters followed William through the old house filled with generations of memories and the promise of generations of memories yet to come. The French doors leading to the back patio were wide open and the gentle breeze teased the gauzy curtains they had drawn over the open doorway.

Lily didn't know why, but this felt like a goodbye. One she wasn't ready for. She reached for her sisters only to find Daisy's hand reaching for hers as Violet moved to Lily's other side and slipped her hand into hers. William moved to the curtains and drew them open for the sisters to walk through. Lily squeezed her sisters' hands and together they moved to say goodbye to a dear friend.

"HAPPY BIRTHDAY!"

Lily and her sisters froze. She was sure her mouth was

open with shock. For standing on the patio was Betsy, along with their husbands. Beyond the patio was the entire population of Keeneston.

Violet was sniffling next to her. Daisy's hand covered her heart as her lower lip trembled. And when her dear husband walked to her and handed her a handkerchief, Lily realized tears were streaming down her cheeks. Lily's mind jumped for joy at the beautiful sight. Chandeliers, colorful lights, balloons, and dresses . . . oh, the beautiful dresses! Her mind wanted to dance, wanted to drink, and wanted to party. Her heart, however, was so full it was overflowing.

Charles took Daisy's hand, John took Lily's, and Anton took Violet's. Together they walked with William and Betsy toward their friends. Kenna, Dani, and Paige stood clasping hands just as Lily, Daisy, and Violet had when they walked through the doors. "Do we have you to thank for this?" Lily asked as she dabbed at her eyes.

They nodded, and in seconds Lily and her sisters were enveloped in hugs, tears, and more love than three childless women could ever imagine. For these *were* their children, their grandchildren, and their great-grandchildren. This was their town. This was their family.

"Oh, dear. They're beautiful," Miss Lily whispered to Sydney as she and her sisters ran their hands softly over the three dresses hanging in the guest room.

Miss Lily's dress was a soft pink, just like her hair. It was in a flapper style with sequins and beaded fringe. Daisy's was a gentle yellow, and Violet's was a light purple. The three dresses were identical except for the color and the beaded embroidery over their heart. Lily's had a lily, Daisy's a daisy, and Violet's a violet.

The three sisters wrapped Sydney in a hug. "You're so talented, and we're so proud of you," Violet told her as they pulled away.

"Thank you. I'm so glad you like them. Do you need any help getting ready?" Sydney asked them.

Lily shook her head. "You go have fun with that husband of yours. We'll be out in just a minute."

They waited for Sydney to leave before squealing their pleasure at their dresses. Violet stopped them, though. "I couldn't get a good feel."

Daisy shook her head. "Me neither. She was as wriggly as a worm on a hook. Lily, were you able to feel Syd's stomach?"

"No, she kept moving. We can't cross her off the list of who's pregnant."

Violet harrumphed with displeasure. "It's our birthday. Whoever is pregnant should tell us. It's the right thing to do."

The Rose sisters agreed as they helped each other into the outfits. Attached to each hanger was a matching headpiece. Lily's was a headband four inches wide made entirely of crystals. Daisy's was a sequined snug-fitting cloche hat, and Violet's was a flowing headscarf decorated with silver thread and violets.

Lily looked into the mirror above the chest at the three of them. Finally. She looked exactly as she felt inside. Young, beautiful, and full of life.

"I have to see myself in a full-length mirror," Violet mumbled as she turned to try to get a good view of herself.

"Yes! I can't wait to see what this fringe looks like at the bottom of the dress," Daisy agreed.

"There's that mirror in the formal sitting room." Lily remembered it from their previous times here.

With a giggle, the three sisters set off for the room on the far side of the house. The soulful sound of Holt Everett singing and people enjoying a party echoed through the empty house.

They pushed the door to the formal sitting room open and flipped on the light. As one, they gasped. Moving slowly toward the object on the floor, Lily nudged it with her toe. "Panties," she whispered.

The three women looked around. "Ohhhhh. This makes me so hoppin' mad." Lily stomped her foot. "First we have the panty dropper and we, of all people, can't figure out who it is. Then we find out someone's pregnant and we can't find out who that is!"

"I think we're slipping in our old age." Daisy crossed her arms over her chest and pouted.

"Or we should be proud," Violet said to them. "After all, we're the ones who taught them how to sneak around."

The three sisters clutched hands and laughed.

The silent couple pressed themselves against the back of the couch as the Rose sisters examined themselves in the mirror. What had they been thinking? That's right, they hadn't been. Looking at the naked man pressed against her, it was easy to see why no thought was necessary. Finally the door closed and they peeked out from behind the couch.

"That was close," he whispered, reaching out to caress a breast.

"Too close. It was exciting as always, but—"

"But it's time for two adults to stop having sex in public like teenagers?" The grin he sent her sent the thoughts skittering out of her head.

"Well—" she hedged, not really wanting to call an end to their fun as she stepped into her dress and pulled it up.

He stepped closer, a hand trailed down her shoulder and under the strap of her dress. "Why don't I give you a reason to keep it up?"

His kiss coincided with the dropping of her dress. Well, what would one more chance at being caught hurt?

12

THE TOWN SANG to them as Zinnia and Poppy presented them with their cake.

Kenna reached over and squeezed her friends' hands as the song ended. "We did it." She smiled as the Rose sisters blew out the candles and everyone clapped.

Looking around the tent, Kenna smiled as the music started up and couples took to the dance floor. DeAndre and Aniyah, Miles and Morgan, Sydney and Deacon, Cody Gray and Addison Rooney, Sienna and Ryan, Pierce and Tammy, Zain and Mila, Riley and Matt, Cade and Annie, Cy and Gemma, Marshall and Katelyn, Ahmed and Bridget, Henry and Neely Grace, Dinky and Chrystal, Noodle and Emma . . . the night was filled with love.

"Sorry we're late."

Kenna turned to the beaming couple unable to keep their hands to themselves. "We're so glad you made it back in time. How was your honeymoon?"

Sophie and Nash looked at each other and Kenna didn't need to know how it was. She was afraid if they told her she'd catch fire from the flames shooting off the newest couple in Keeneston.

"Hey, I didn't know Jackson was in town. And look, he brought Lucas Sharpe and Talon Bainbridge. Let's go say hi after we see my parents," Sophie said, taking in the crowd.

"Oh my gosh," Dani whispered as the couple walked off.

"I know, right?" Paige sighed. "And look at our husbands."

Kenna and Dani looked across to the bar and found their husbands looking dangerously handsome as they laughed while they got drinks. The song ended and the women and men separated from the dance floor. "Did you get to see Sophie yet?" Kenna asked Annie when she joined them.

"I did. They had a great honeymoon. She's happy, and as her mother, that's all I've ever wanted." Annie looked around the group. "What are you all staring at?"

"Our husbands," they sighed. Annie turned around and saw why. "Damn, ladies. We did good."

"Cheers to that," Morgan said as she lifted a glass of Rose sisters' iced tea.

"To our husbands, and to Gabe finding love next," Dani toasted.

"Cheers!"

"Our parents are wasted," Cassidy Davies said, looking at her father, Pierce, trying to limbo. "It's so embarrassing."

"Lighten up, Cass. Have some iced tea," her brother, Dylan, told her, shoving a glass of special iced tea into her hand.

"I'm only twenty." Cassidy tried to hand the drink back to her brother.

"Then it's about damn time. Loosen up, sis." Dylan crossed his muscular arms over his thick chest. The edges of a tattoo could be seen peeking out from the end of his tight, short-sleeved T-shirt.

"Time for what?" Jace asked as he joined his brother, sisters, and the rest of the Davies cousins.

"For Cassidy to have a drink and lighten up," Dylan told him.

"Yeah, I kinda agree with Dylan."

"Piper," Cassidy pleaded turning to her sister.

"Do you. Whatever that is. But if you're going to have a drink, you better do it now because Holt Everett just put on some recorded music and is walking this way." Piper saw the young Nashville star walking toward them with his eyes glued to Cassidy.

"He touches you and I'll rip his arms off and shove them down his throat," Dylan growled.

"And I'll hold him down," Jace smirked.

"I'm so glad I'm the oldest," Piper muttered as Holt braved his way through the wall of brothers to ask Cassidy to dance.

"Ava," Jace called out to Noodle and Dr. Emma's daughter. He stepped away from the crowd and asked the medical student to dance.

Landon, Kale, Porter, and Parker stood off to the side, drinking. "I so don't trust them when they're all together," Sophie said from behind the group. Those four were known to get in a little trouble. Miss Lily had broken a few brooms over them in the past.

"Sophie!" her friends and family called out as they greeted her and Nash with hugs and "welcome backs."

"And I know what you mean," Abby said, eyeing her younger brother who tossed his head back and laughed.

"And look at our brothers. They're so up to something," Reagan said as Riley nodded her head. Porter and Parker were definitely thinking of something. When they eyed a group of Belles, they found the answer.

"It must run in the family," Layne teased as Reagan smacked her arm.

"Hey y'all," Jackson's deep voice said, interrupting Layne's teasing. "Do you remember Lucas and Talon? We have a few days off. When I told them I was coming home, they jumped in the car before I could kick them out."

The other men rolled their eyes at their partner. Talon, Lucas, and Jackson were on the FBI's hostage rescue team together and were as close as brothers. Paige and Cole had taken them in, and they considered Ryan to be their older brother and watched out for Greer as if she were their younger sister. Subsequently, the entire town had just adopted the two FBI agents. Talon, having been raised in Australia, had women swooning with his accent. Lucas was from Alaska and caused them to laugh with his love of polar bears and his inability to get cold.

"Hey, good to see you two again," Wyatt's smooth country voice said as he shook hands with Lucas and Talon. "And, sis, I thought I'd warn you that the mailman was complaining about another package he had to deliver to your house. Because of the party tonight, he'll bring it by tomorrow. It's from your father-in-law."

Sydney tossed back her head and groaned. "Deacon!" she yelled as she went in search of her husband.

Wyatt laughed as Carter shook his head. "It's not funny. I've seen what my mom is doing to my sister and it scares the crap out of me."

"Well, if Sienna would hurry up and get pregnant, she could take the pressure off all of us," Riley called out across the group to Sienna who responded with a single-finger gesture.

"Hello, Abby. "

"Nolan!" Abby smiled and turned to hug her first real boyfriend. They'd broken up in high school but had remained friends.

"Want to catch up over a dance?" Nolan asked.

"I'd love to," Abby smiled and flashed her bright blue eyes at Nolan as they headed for the dance floor.

"And you two don't have a problem with that?" Ariana asked Jackson and Dylan as she and her brother Gabe joined them.

Jackson and Dylan looked at each other and then to Ariana with identical blank looks.

"Abby can do whatever she wants. No business of mine," Dylan said casually.

"Yeah, we're just friends. Like you and Kale. Do you have a problem with him dancing with—" Jackson looked out on the dance floor and sucked in a breath.

"Shit," Dylan cringed.

"What?" Ariana asked as Gabe covered her eyes.

"You don't want to see this. You're too young." Ariana shoved her brother away and looked toward Kale.

"Eww! He's dancing with Nikki Canter."

The whole group gasped as Nikki slithered her body against Kale's.

"She's, like, old," Ariana stuttered as Nikki's skirt rose higher and higher up her thighs.

"She's just a couple years older than you, and I don't think Kale cares. Do you care?" Gabe asked. "If you do, I'll beat the crap out of him."

Ariana rolled her eyes. "No, we're just friends."

"See," Dylan and Jackson said with their arms crossed over their chests.

"Point taken," Ariana grumbled.

"Come on, princess, let's dance." Wyatt bent at the waist in an elaborate bow.

Ariana snickered. It was almost enough to make up for the fact he called her princess. Ari hated that. She liked being just Ariana with all her friends. "My pleasure, kind sir."

"My, my, my," Miss Lily clucked. "Zain is being rather attentive to his wife."

"She's not pregnant," John told her.

"How? You old billy goat. At some point you will have to tell me how you know these things."

"She may not be pregnant now, but by the way Zain is dancing with her, she could be very soon," Miss Daisy said as the group nodded.

The song ended and the two came toward the main table. Lily waved Poppy and those two FBI boys over to their table. "Can you get me a pitcher of Rose sisters' tea to go?"

Poppy sputtered before words came out. "You want a whole pitcher? I don't think that's such a good idea."

Miss Lily waved her off. "Not for me. For Zain and Mila."

"Oh, sure." Poppy quickly disappeared to fetch the container full of bourbon-spiked iced tea.

"Miss Lily, Miss Daisy, Miss Violet, happy birthday." Zain leaned forward and kissed each of their cheeks before Violet grabbed Zain and buried his head in her bosom.

"Dear, you don't want to be responsible for the death of a prince," her husband, Anton, said dryly as he shook his head. Violet let go of Zain's head as she patted his face.

"We're sorry, but we have to leave a little early. We're heading on vacation for a couple weeks. We thought we couldn't be ready until tomorrow, but we just received notice everything is ready for us to take off," Mila told them as she followed suit with the kisses to the cheeks. "But we wanted to wish you a very happy birthday before we left."

"Well, thank you, my dears. It's so good to get away every now and then." *And make babies*, Lily thought.

"We'll see you as soon as we get back. I can't wait to hear what you got for your birthday." Mila looked over at the six tables full of gifts.

"Dear, we'll still be opening them when you return," Miss Daisy said dryly.

"And we have a little gift for you, too," Miss Lily said as Poppy handed her the canister filled with spiked tea. "For the plane ride to wherever you're going."

Zain took the canister and opened it. He took a sip and almost coughed. "It's a strong batch."

"Just for you two," Miss Lily winked. "Enjoy it and don't do anything I wouldn't do."

Daisy and Violet snorted. "Which means you can do whatever you want because there's nothing Lily won't do," Daisy snickered as Violet tried not to laugh but lost all control.

"You won't believe this time in high school—"

"Violet!" Lily snapped, causing her sisters to just laugh louder.

They were still lovingly bickering as Zain put his arm around his wife and led her from the tent. "You know, this might be the best gift the Rose sisters could have given us."

Mila chuckled as she slipped her hand into his. "How's that?"

"Because I have so many ideas for how to pleasure you

all the way until we touch down in the Bahamas. And the iced tea is a good way to get you to let me do what's on page 127 of this book I've found."

Mila laughed but didn't say no. Zain did a mental high-five as he slipped his hand to his wife's bottom and gently squeezed as they disappeared into the shadows of the farm to catch a ride back to Desert Farm.

13

GREER STARED in disbelief at her brothers, Jackson and Ryan, along with Lucas and Talon. Sienna had left them to talk to Sydney and Layne, so Greer had no one else to help her talk common sense into these guys.

"I don't think I like this idea," Ryan said slowly.

"Yeah, it's one thing to be in the FBI with my brother, but my sister? I don't like the idea either," Jackson said, standing shoulder to shoulder with Ryan.

"Me either," Talon told her. "Do you know what the guys are like in the FBI?"

"Assholes," Lucas answered for her. "Totally not worthy of you."

Greer rolled her hazel eyes laced with silver slivers. "So what you're saying is all y'all are a bunch of assholes?"

"Yes," Ryan answered before stopping. "No."

"What we're saying is—" Jackson started.

"If you say it's because I'm a girl, I'm going to kick you in the balls."

"Wait a sec," Talon cut in. "Are you just thinking about it or are you being recruited?"

Greer didn't answer, which was an answer within itself.

"Hi, Greer," Andy said, having no idea what a tense conversation he was entering. "Hi, guys."

Andy was the same height as Greer, and she'd been friends with him forever. They were practically family. Dinky was his father and Aunt Annie's cousin, Chrystal, was his mother. Unfortunately, that meant he was short with shocking orange-red hair and freckles. Fortunately, he was also one of the nicest guys in town and none of the men she was talking to now would dare be rude to him.

"What's up, Andy?" Ryan asked.

"I'm trying something new. Thinking of taking my career in a different direction," Andy told them.

"Apparently my sister is also," Jackson said tightly.

"Oh, great. I can't wait to hear about it," Andy smiled at her. "Do you want to dance, Greer?"

"I'd love to, Andy." Greer laced her hand through his arm and managed not to stick her tongue out at her brothers as she walked to the dance floor.

Reagan watched him dancing and cursed herself for being a chicken. She just didn't feel like putting up with her father like Riley and Matt did so she'd pleaded with him to keep their relationship a secret. Though it wasn't really a relationship. Or maybe it was. It was pretty undefined and that was all her fault.

"What's wrong?"

Damn that twin thing. Riley was by her side with questions in her eyes.

"Nothing. Just wishing I had someone to dance with."

"I'm sure Porter or Parker would dance with you."

Reagan looked at her sister like she was the dumbest

person in the world. "I'm not dancing with my little brothers. Besides, they're already dancing with a couple of Belles." Sadly, Reagan had already thought about that.

"What about Cody? He doesn't have a partner, and he's looking your way."

"Cody looks everyone's way," Reagan said with a slight smile. The newest deputy was a great guy. He just wasn't one who was ready to settle down yet. And at twenty-five, why should he? But he seemed like a teenager to her twenty-nine years.

"But desperate times," Reagan muttered, smiling at Cody, which was enough to send him moving in their direction.

"You know," Riley started to say. "If you just outed yourself and your secret, then you wouldn't be without a dance partner."

"And I'd suffer the same way you and Matt do at Dad's hand. When your father is an ex-spy, it really messes with your love life."

"At least I have Matt beside me and in my bed to deal with it without trying to hide it," Riley said under her breath as Cody approached.

"Hi, Riley. Where's the boss?" Cody asked.

"Right here." Matt came up behind Cody and held out his hand to Riley. "I was coming to ask my wife to dance."

"And I was going to ask Reagan if she'd like to dance." Cody smiled happily at her. He'd be a good distraction because her sister had just given her too much to think about.

"I'd love to," Reagan smiled.

Cody put his arm around her and she let her thoughts go. For tonight, she was just going to enjoy herself and keep her little secret to herself.

"Firemen are so hot," Nikki purred as she ran her hand down Colton's chest.

Colton smiled at her, knowing it would be rude not to. "So you've said."

"I'm so sorry to interrupt, but I need to have a word with my brother," Sophie said so sweetly that Nikki flinched. Apparently the memories of their previous encounters were still vivid.

"Of course." Nikki turned to Colton and winked. "And I'll see you later tonight. You won't believe what I can do with a pole."

"She scares me," Colton said, shaking his head and watching Nikki walk away. "Can I borrow your taser? You know, for safety?"

"What taser?" Sophie blinked innocently.

"Eventually I'll get it out of you. Welcome home, by the way, Mrs. Dagher."

"Thanks, little brother," Sophie teased. "Mom filled me in on you starting Keeneston's first fire station."

"Yeah. I'm pretty excited about it. I have a construction grant, but I still need to raise more money for equipment."

Sophie smiled. "Can I drive the fire truck if I pay for it?"

"If you buy one, I'll put your freaking name on it."

"I wanted to tell you I'm proud of you. It's a great idea, and Nash and I will help in anyway you need us. I can do a fund-raiser and donate some money. Whatever you need."

Colton gave his big sister a hug. "Thanks, Soph. That means a lot. I see the Rose sisters are free. I'm going to wish them a happy birthday and then we can talk about that money you just mentioned," he joked.

Colton shook Nash's hand and headed for the front

table. Nash slid his arm around his new wife. "As fun as this is, I think it's time to head home. It's been almost a day since you were naked and in my arms," he whispered, causing his lips to brush seductively along her neck.

"One more dance," Sophie said as she reached for Nash's hand. "Even the Rose sisters are going to dance."

"I can't deny my wife anything," Nash joked as they headed to the full dance floor.

~

"To Miss Lily, Miss Daisy, and Miss Violet!" Holt called out as everyone raised their glass and toasted the Rose sisters. "A special song that will be on my first album whenever it comes out."

The crowd cheered as the dance floor filled to capacity. She watched as couples danced between tables to the slow song about small-town living and loving. The Rose sisters danced with their husbands in the center of the room surrounded by the people of Keeneston.

"I want you again. Now."

Her breath escaped her as the deep, low voice came from behind her.

"Yes," she said accepting the challenge. Well, they could always quit tomorrow.

~

Miss Lily sat looking out over the crowd. These people were there to celebrate their birthday, and she loved them all so dearly. She reached for her sisters' hands and leaned toward them to be heard over the music. "Happy birthday, dear sisters."

"I don't know how they'll top it next year," Daisy smirked.

"'Cause we're not ready to go anywhere yet. Even if Florida does sound nice," Violet said with determination.

"We have too much work left to do. There are far too many people needing our help. Colton with his fire department, Zain and Mila with their pregnancy—remind me to tell Zinnia to put some of those special herbs into their meals for the next couple of months. And there's a whole lot of young people looking for love," Lily said, looking over the crowd.

"I thought we were retired from matchmaking?" Daisy snickered as they all laughed at the joke. That was just something they told their husbands.

"Bless their hearts, these women need our help. It's our civic duty," Violet said looking out at Kenna, Dani, and Paige dancing with their husbands.

"They're getting better, though. With the right nudges here and there, we'll turn them into professional matchmakers soon enough. But first, I got us a present." Lily smiled as she reached into her bag and handed an envelope to each sister. They tore into them and grinned.

"Hang gliding!" Violet gasped.

"With them?" Daisy asked, pointing to the handsome young men on the cover of the brochure.

"You betcha," Lily smiled. "We may be getting older, but we still have a lot of living left."

Daisy raised her glass. "To us."

"To our first . . ." Violet paused not wanting to say how old they really were. "So many years."

"And to many more," Lily toasted.

THE END

Bluegrass Series

Bluegrass State of Mind

Risky Shot

Dead Heat

Bluegrass Brothers

Bluegrass Undercover

Rising Storm

Secret Santa: A Bluegrass Series Novella

Acquiring Trouble

Relentless Pursuit

Secrets Collide

Final Vow

Bluegrass Singles

All Hung Up

Bluegrass Dawn

The Perfect Gift

The Keeneston Roses

Forever Bluegrass Series

Forever Entangled

Forever Hidden

Forever Betrayed

Forever Driven

Forever Secret

Forever Concealed - coming September 19, 2017

<u>Women of Power Series</u>

Chosen for Power

Built for Power

Fashioned for Power

Destined for Power

<u>*Web of Lies Series*</u>

Whispered Lies

Rogue Lies

Shattered Lies - coming October 19, 2017

ABOUT THE AUTHOR

Kathleen Brooks is a New York Times, Wall Street Journal, and USA Today bestselling author. Kathleen's stories are romantic suspense featuring strong female heroines, humor, and happily-ever-afters. Her Bluegrass Series and follow-up Bluegrass Brothers Series feature small town charm with quirky characters that have captured the hearts of readers around the world.

Kathleen is an animal lover who supports rescue organizations and other non-profit organizations such as Friends and Vets Helping Pets whose goals are to protect and save our four-legged family members.

Email Notice of New Releases
kathleen-brooks.com/new-release-notifications
Kathleen's Website
www.kathleen-brooks.com
Facebook Page
www.facebook.com/KathleenBrooksAuthor
Twitter
www.twitter.com/BluegrassBrooks
Goodreads
www.goodreads.com

CPSIA information can be obtained
at www.ICGtesting.com
Printed in the USA
LVOW12s0855081017
551660LV00002B/369/P